WHEN?

("So The House of Israel shall know that I AM JEHOVAH
their GOD from That Day and forward."   Ezekiel 39:22)

A prophetical novel of the very near future

by

H. BEN JUDAH

*"Sanctify them through Thy Truth:
Thy Word is Truth." John 17:17.*

With the exception of public personages mentioned, all characters in this
book are purely fictitious. Resemblance to any persons living or dead are
therefore entirely coincidental.

CONTENTS

PREFACE.

This book, as the reader will find, is no literary masterpiece; nor was it written for the purpose of being one.

Its sole object is to bring to the notice of the public the source of our economic, financial, health, and other troubles.

Do not let the reader be deceived into believing that this book is anti-Semitic. Actually it is just the opposite, the writer himself being of Semitic Judah, and therefore wishing to point out that there are two types of so-called Jews, the real Semitic Jew and the Ashkenazim so-called Jew who is a convert to Judaism only, ostensibly by religion, but not by blood.

If the reader were to accept Mohammedanism, would this make him an Arab or a Turk, the national religion of whose countries is Mohammedanism? Of course not. The writer knows several British people who have accepted Mohammedanism as their religion, but who have still kept their British nationality and name.

Why then, should the Ashkenazim so-called Jew, as well as the other converts to Judaism, call themselves Jews? Why should the Zionist Party, the great majority of whose leaders are Ashkenazim or other converts to Judaism only (although in many cases their ancestors accepted Judaism many centuries ago) claim the Holy Land? This book endeavours to explain their reasons.

Professor Lothrop Stoddard, the very eminent authority on Ethnology, published an article in *Forum* some years ago in which he stated:

"There are two sharply contrasted types of *so-called* Jews."

(1) "Ashkenazim: Those from Eastern Europe. Short in stature, *round-headed*, with typical Jewish noses."

(2) "Sephardim: Those from the Mediterranean. Slender in

figure, *long-headed*, with fine-cut noses, an harmonic **type.**"

His article further states: "Mankind is divided into two great races, the Dolicocephalic (long-skulled) and the Brachycephalic (round-skulled). The Ashkenazim are round-skulled, whilst the real Semitic Jews are of the long-skulled race. Racially they are as far apart as the Poles, and their (Ashkenazim) claim to Palestine on historic grounds is therefore worthless."

His article concludes that the Ashkenazim are neither Jewish nor Semitic; that they can be summed up as a mongrel breed of minor Asiatic races, with a strong admixture of Turko-Mongol blood, and that there is a profound cleavage between them and the real Semitic Jew.

(It might be pointed out that King Herod, who massacred the "Innocents of Bethlehem," was an Idumean, as were his followers, and the Idumeans were a Turko-Mongol breed.)

In spite of the findings of Professor Stoddard, it is the Ashkenazim who, through the Zionist Party which they appear to control, are claiming the Holy Land on historic grounds. As Professor Stoddard states, their claims are entirely false.

Our Lord Jesus Christ (Rev. 1: 1) twice warns us, stating in Rev. 2: *9*, "I know the blasphemy of them which SAY they are Jews, and are not, but are the synagogue of Satan"; and again in Rev. 3: *9* (again note the "*9*" of Judgement) warns us of, "them of the synagogue of Satan, which SAY they are Jews, and are NOT, but do lie." Further, Isaiah, also in 3: *9*, when referring to the inhabitants of Jerusalem, tells us, "the show of their countenance doth witness against them."

But what does it witness? Apparently it witnesses what Our Lord stated, that they are NOT Jews. It would appear that the "show of their countenance" refers to the round-skull and *so-called* typical Jewish nose, which Professor Stoddard states are signs of the Ashkenazim, and which he also states are signs that they are neither Jewish nor Semitic. Hence the Bible and science entirely agree about the Ashkenazim.

When the reader understands these points, he will realize that this book is not anti-Semitic, but rather pro-Semitic, as it warns only of the Ashkenazim and their plans for world control, and endeavours to point out that the true Semitic Jew is not responsible.

The reader of the newspapers who looks beneath the surface of what he reads, can now see Gog's confederacy being formed, as prophesied in Ezekiel, chapter 38, and this will be much more apparent within the next few months. How soon that attack will start is a different matter.

However, Gog's attack when it comes, is God's plan for the awakening of His people Israel from their blindness and, although we shall doubtless have to go through some very trying situations, there is nothing to fear, appearances to the contrary. God has said, "Thou (Israel) art My servant; I have chosen thee, and NOT cast thee away:" (Isa. 41 : *9*, note the "*9*" of Judgement), so we can trust firmly in that promise until His purpose in Gog's attack is accomplished and, "So the House of Israel shall know that I AM JEHOVAH their GOD from that day and forward." (Ezek, 39 : 22.)

The writer's attempted interpretation of the Scriptural events to take place are in all cases taken from the prophecies given us in the Bible. Whilst in the majority of the cases only one reference is given in this book, a study of the prophecies shows that in most cases the various events are corroborated by more than one prophet, although the exact wording may be of a slightly different significance, due often to the translators.

In the Fenton translation, considered by many to be the most accurate of the translations, Ezekiel 38: 17 tells us, "Thus says the Mighty Lord: 'You (Gog) are the one of whom I spoke in *former times* by means of My servants the prophets of Israel, who proclaimed in the period of their life that I would bring *you* upon them.' (Israel.)"

We can, therefore, see that the prophecies of Isaiah, Jeremiah, Joel, Hosea, Amos, Zephaniah, Haggai, Zechariah, and particularly chapters 38 and 39 of Ezekiel all refer to Gog's impending attack; whilst Daniel 12: 12 refers to the final result of that attack.

From a study of all the prophecies, it would appear that Gog's attack is the signal that the curtain has gone up for the final act of the "Times of the Gentiles" (Luke 21: 24): that the next scene will be Armageddon, to be followed by the "Sign of the Son of Man" (Matt. 24: 30), which in turn will be followed by the return of Our Lord Jesus Christ, and the setting up of His Millenial Kingdom of peace, blessing, health, and prosperity for the whole House of Israel, and for all others who accept Him.

Let Israel, therefore, take the advice of His Majesty King George VI, who in his Christmas broadcast at the beginning of the present war, said, "Place your hand in the hand of God." Let us take this good advice, and He will lead us unafraid into the Kingdom of God on earth.

(Signed) H. BEN JUDAH.

April 15, 1944.

CHAPTER 1.

Gog Strikes.

Brian Benjamin sat at his desk with his head bowed. The blow of which he had warned his Chief had fallen. Gog had attacked Palestine a few days earlier, without giving any warning, and the British Commonwealth of Nations sat back aghast at the sabotage and destruction which had been caused by Gog's Fifth Column throughout the Commonwealth.

There had been sabotage in the arsenals, war plants, and other industries which would be required for the war effort. Sand had been found in the oils and greases used in our armoured vehicles and tanks, as well as in naval and aircraft machinery. Sugar had been placed in the carburetors and fuel tanks of our aircraft, armoured vehicles, transport, and other motors. Explosions had occurred in the arsenals and in the magazines of our warships. Fires of incendiary origin were everywhere.

Perhaps the gravest danger had been from Gog's insidious propaganda in the armed services, and particularly amongst some branches of organized labour. This propaganda had resulted in a small percentage of those in the services being half-hearted in their allegiance, whilst members of several unions had "walked out," refusing to work against Gog.

Adherents of Gog were to be found even in the "Mother of Parliaments" and in government departments, and although those who openly looked forward to a Magogian victory were few in number, it was impossible to tell how far his propaganda had been successful, and how many had been poisoned by it, and were secretly working against their King and country.

Brian was in "Intelligence," in which he had served for twelve years, after retiring from the army with the rank of lieutenant-colonel.

He had recently returned from a secret mission to Meshech, where from various agents he had learned that Gog was making secret plans to attack Palestine. He had further learned that it was at the request of the Zionist Jews that Gog was to attack, and that the Zionists had promised their fullest co-operation in the matter.

All this he had reported in detail to his chief, who in turn had reported the matter to the Foreign Office, but so far as he was aware no action nor precautions had been taken by the government.

As he sat there despondently, the phone rang and his Chief told him to report to him at once.

On his arrival at his Chief's office, Brian found the latter staring out of the window in deep thought. He turned to Brian and said, "Morning, Benjamin; sit down." Then continued, "This is bad, very bad. How bad, the public, and I think the government as a whole, little realize." He paused, then asked, "By the way, Benjamin, aren't you of Jewish extraction? I think I remember seeing it on your papers some time ago."

"Yes, sir," replied Brian. "Both my father and mother were of Sephardim Jewish blood, but we have been converted to Christianity for many generations."

"Perhaps," said his Chief, "under those circumstances you could tell me why the Jews have arranged with Gog to attack Palestine. Is it entirely on account of the British Government's White Paper, as a result of which Jewish immigration into Palestine was to be stopped in March, 1944, or have they other and deeper reasons?"

Brian thought for a moment, and replied, "Well you see, sir, it is entirely the Zionist Party which is involved in the matter. That party consists almost wholly of Ashkenazim Jews, with practically no membership amongst the Sephardim. The Sephardim have never laid claim to the ownership of Palestine, as from their ancient records they realize that they are only the descendants of a remnant of the Tribe of Judah, whilst that whole tribe was only one of the thirteen Tribes of

Israel. Although Israel is usually referred to as having twelve tribes, the Tribe of Joseph was divided into two tribes, Ephraim and Manasseh, so actually there were thirteen tribes."

"However, I know little of the Jewish question as my people have been Christianized for many generations, and consequently have been rather out of touch with Jewish affairs. On the other hand, I have a cousin who is a prominent figure in Jewish affairs, Samuel Josephus, and who has studied that question very deeply. Fortunately I am on very good terms with him, and if you wish I shall see him at once and endeavour to obtain the information you require, and any other information I can, from him."

"Good," said his Chief. "The Foreign Office is very worried as to Jewish reactions in this country, and wish to ascertain what form the Jewish propaganda will take. As you are aware, our newspapers, financial system, and to a certain extent our broadcasting system are greatly under Jewish control, and consequently they are in a position to deeply influence public opinion in this country. The great majority of the people do not think for themselves, but believe what they read in the papers or hear broadcast to them. Better get busy, Old Boy, and see what information you can gather from this prominent cousin of yours."

"Very well, sir," Brian said, "I'll start at once."

He telephoned, found that his cousin, Samuel Josephus, was in and could see him at once, so lost no time in reaching his office.

On being shown in to Samuel's office, he explained his business, and waited whilst his cousin thought the matter over.

Finally Samuel said, "Well Brian, you have asked questions which cannot be answered shortly. I know that you have never taken any interest in Jewish matters. Have you ever studied the question of who the Jews are?"

"No," replied Brian, "I can't say that I have. Of course I know that the Jews are the remnant of Judah, as signified by their name, and include a few of the Tribe of Benjamin and a proportion of the Tribe of Levi, but that the main part of the Tribe of Judah is 'lost' somewhere, no one knows where, and that the Ten Tribes of Israel, who after the division of the Nation of Israel were the Northern Kingdom with capital at Samaria, are also 'lost,' and that no one knows what happened to them after the Assyrians deported them into Medeo-Persia[1] about 700 B.C."

"Yes, of course," replied Samuel. "But what I was driving at was as to whom the present day Jews are?"

Brian said, "No, I fear that I don't know much about that, except that we are Sephardim, whilst there are other Jews called Ashkenazim. Also, I recently discovered that nearly all the Zionist Party are Ashkenazim."

"Yes," replied his cousin. "You are right in those points, except that I do not know of any Sephardim at all amongst the leaders of the Zionists, although there may be some amongst its members. Also, did you ever realize that the Ashkenazim are not Jews at all, except by religion, and that they are not even Semitic?"

"No! Is that so?" said Brian. "Well then who are they?"

Samuel replied, "It's a long story which I have studied for years. I first became interested in the question years ago when I noticed that the Ashkenazim were ethnologically different from ourselves, the Sephardim. The Ashkenazim have a head differently shaped from ours, whilst nearly all of them have hooked noses. In cartoons the Jew is always depicted as having a hooked nose. I have yet to find a Jew of true Sephardim blood with a noticeably hooked nose, although some have a slightly hooked one; but many British people not of Jewish blood also have slightly hooked noses, which they term aquiline. The Sephardim in nearly all cases have a straight well-cut nose."

"From the cartoons, if they represent public opinion, it would appear that the Gentiles consider the Ashkenazim to be the real Jew, which is not the case."

[1] II Kings, 17: 6.

"The question of who the Ashkenazim are got me so interested that I employed several eminent ethnologists at my own expense to study the question and report on it to me."

"All these ethnologists, although working separately and unknown to each other, came to similar findings in their reports, a summing up of which reports I shall read to you."

Samuel produced a paper from his desk, and read the following extract:

"There are two types of so-called Jews.

(1) Ashkenazim from Eastern Europe; round-skulled, short in stature, with typical Jewish noses.

(2) Sephardim, from the Mediterranean, long-skulled, with fine-cut noses, tall and slender, an harmonic figure."

He folded up the paper, and continued, "They then go on to point out that there are two great races into which mankind is divided, the Brachycephalic (round-skulled) and the Dolicocephalic (long-skulled), and that the Ashkenazim are of the former race, whilst we Sephardim are of the latter."

"All these ethnologists conclude that the Ashkenazim are a minor Asiatic mongrel breed, with a strong admixture of Turko-Mongol blood, but that the Sephardim is the true Jew of Semitic blood.[1] Quite interesting, isn't it?"

"Yes, indeed," said Brian, "but then who are the Ashkenazim? Are they by any chance some of the 'lost' Ten Tribes?"

"No," Samuel replied, "the ethnologists prove conclusively that they are of the round-headed Alpine race, whereas the true Semitic Jew, and naturally the remainder of Israel, are of the long-headed Mediterranean race. No; so far as I have been able to ascertain from our Rabbis and their records, the Ashkenazim are the descendants of the Herodians. As you will perhaps remember, Caesar Augustus appointed Herod as King of Judea whilst the Jews were subject to Rome. Now, Herod and his followers were Idumeans, and the Idumeans

---

[1] Prof. Stoddard in *Forum*, March, 1926.

were of Turko-Mongol stock, and had the typical so-called Jewish nose of the Ashkenazim."

"In that case," said Brian, "the Ashkenazim Zionist Party have no claims whatever to Palestine, other than the fact that a Roman Emperor appointed for a short time one of their number as a tributary king over the Jews when the latter were subject to Rome."

"You are quite correct," said his cousin. "Their claims are entirely false, and further it is the Ashkenazim who are always raising the cry of 'anti-Semitism' in the press and over the broadcasting system whenever their claims to Palestine are opposed, whereas as you are now aware, they are not even of Semitic origin at all."

"Now Semitic means descended from Sem, the son of Noah, which in English is spelled Shem. This would include many nations besides Israel, but the Zionist 'scholarship' has tried to make it mean Jews only, which is entirely wrong."

"Shem, or Sem, had five sons and many grandsons[1], and naturally all their descendants would be Semitic. Abraham was a descendant of one of Shem's sons, and his grandson Jacob had twelve sons, of which Judah was one; whilst of Judah the Jewish remnant was only a very small percentage. Naturally all Israel are Semitic. This shows the absurdity of the Zionists' interpretation of the word 'Semitic.' "

"Hitler made the statement that it is the Ashkenazim Jew who is the international financier, Communist, and trouble-maker generally. From my own researches into their activities, I am in that one point inclined to agree with Hitler."

"A very interesting situation arose during the controversy as to whether the Zionists should be given the Holy Land."

"The leaders of the three parties concerned, that is the Sephardim who laid no claim to the ownership of the land: the Zionists who claimed the land; and the Arabs, who protested against the wholesale immigration of the Zionists into the land, which large immigration was entirely contrary to the

---
[1] Gen. 10: 22.

terms of the Balfour Declaration, as it promised to protect the Arabs, all agreed to visit the late Rev. Pascoe Goard. The latter had studied the Israel and Jewish question for years, and had probably more knowledge of the rights of the question than any living man.''

"The leaders put up their cases to Goard, and asked for his decision. Goard turned to Lord Firemountain, leader of the Sephardim Party, and said, 'You are quite correct in your assumption that such of the Sephardim as wish to live in the Holy Land should be allowed to do so, provided that they do not assail the rights of the Arabs. You are further correct in your statement that the Semitic Jews, that is the Sephardim, realize that they are the descendants of only a small remnant of Judah, the whole of whom were only some ten per cent of the whole House of Israel.' "

"He then turned to the leader of the Zionist Party, a man high in both international and British financial circles, as he had also been during the First Great War when some very nasty rumours were prevalent as to his pro-German activities, he being of German antecedents although he had adopted a British name, and said to him, 'Even if you Zionists were of Semitic or Jewish blood, WHICH YOU ARE NOT, you would have the right to only a very small portion of the Holy Land, which belongs to the whole House of Israel. As it is, you have no right by blood or otherwise to any part of the land whatsoever, as your claims are false.' "

"Goard then turned to Ibn Saud, leader of the Arabs, and said, 'The Arabs are the descendants of Ishmael, who was given the right by Jehovah to "Dwell in the presence of all his brethren,"[1] who are Israel. The Arabs therefore have the right to dwell unmolested in the Holy Land, but have no claim to its ownership.' "

"It is an historical fact," Samuel continued, "that Ibn Saud was so impressed by these decisions that he asked Goard to write a manifesto, of which Ibn Saud had several million copies

[1] Gen. 16: 12.

printed at his own expense, which he at once sent to the Arabs.
The result was that the Holy War which the Arabs were pre-
paring was called off, and it is probable that the British White
Paper stopping Zionist immigration into Palestinee was the
result."

"In spite of the absurdity of their claims to the Holy Land,
the Zionists have continued to use every possible method of
propaganda and subterfuge to have the British Government
cede Palestine to them, but the government have tried to grant
justice to the Arabs, and have denied the Zionists' false claims."

"It is a most unfortunate thing that the public do not realize
the difference between the international so-called Jew, whose
loyalty is always to the Zionist Party and not to the country
of his adoption, and the true Sephardim Jew of Semitic blood,
the great majority of whom are truly loyal to the country in
which they live."

"You see," he continued, "the Ashkenazim work by underground methods, by intrigue, by bribery and corruption, or
by any means by which they can obtain their ends. The Gentiles
do not realize any distinction between the Sephardim and Ashkenazim, in fact very, very few of them even realize that there
are two races of so-called Jews. Consequently the Sephardim
are unfairly included in the opprobrium of the Gentiles against
the Jew for the unfair dealings of the Ashkenazim."

"However," he continued after a short pause, "I think that
with the information which you now possess, we can discuss the
points about which you visited me."

"You may tell your Chief," Samuel continued slowly, "that
he can trust the Sephardim fully. They are absolutely loyal
to the British Empire, from whom they have received freedom
and justice. As you know, I hold a prominent position amongst
the Sephardim, as do my colleagues, all of whom hold opinions
in this matter similar to my own. You may therefore assure
your Chief, and those above him, that they may count on us
to do anything possible to help them in any way they may wish."

"I wish," he continued slowly, "that I could give a similar assurance for the Ashkenazim part of Jewry, but I cannot do so."

"The Ashkenazim," he continued harshly, "are out for world-control. Are you aware that Gog is entirely controlled by the Ashkenazim? That some 83 per cent of Gog's district commissioners are of Ashkenazim extraction? That five out of six of those who constitute Gog's Grand Council are also Ashkenazim, whilst about the same proportion of all their government officials are of that race?"

"No," said Brian, "I was not aware that they held such a strong control, although 'Intelligence' has been aware for years that Gog was under their influence. I knew, of course, as I told you, that the Zionist Party had arranged with Gog to attack and seize Palestine for them, but I was not aware that they were all so 'hand-in-glove' with each other. Perhaps you could give me some further information as to the ideas underlying their actions, as it is all very useful to my Chief?"

"Do you know anything about the 'synagogue of Satan?'" Samuel said.

"No," replied Brian, "except that in my work I have heard that there is such a secret organization, and one of my former commanding officers told me that he had spent twenty years in trying to trace their activities and organization. He said that they secretly controlled our financial system and were responsible for all of our financial and economic troubles."

"That is quite correct. They do control the financial system," said his cousin. "There is little doubt of that. It was they who were responsible for having the old British laws against interest and usury, which actually are synonymous according to the best dictionaries, repealed. They also engineered, of course under cover, the Bank Charter Act in 1844. By means of this they were enabled to gain control of the financial system, and as a result have been able to institute methods of compounding interest and issuing credits by which they have caused the national debt to grow to staggering pro-portions. If they are allowed to continue their present methods taxes will grow to such a percentage of income that industry will be unable to survive. This I believe to be their object so far as the democratic nations are concerned. At present the nation and government are subservient to the international financier."

"However, although important, the financial end is not the most important at the present time, and in order to understand its ideas and workings I must give you a short outline of the history of the 'synagogue of Satan.'"

"Nimrod, who shortly after the Flood founded the ancient Babel, later called Babylon, is usually considered to have been its founder. However, from some ancient records which I dis-covered in Jerusalem, where I lived for some years during my researches, it would appear that it was Cain, the son of Eve, who founded that synagogue."

"According to these old records, called Targums, the object of the society was to work for Satan against Jehovah. Its efforts were so successful that, with the exception of Noah, all mankind appears to have come under the control of Satan. Noah's line of descent had apparently alone been kept pure from the Canaanite strain of blood."

"Unfortunately one of Noah's sons, Ham, had married Naamah,[1] who was a descendant of Cain,[2] and thus the contami-nated blood was brought through the Flood, and again carried on through the line of Ham, whose grandson Nimrod refounded Babylon, and apparently reorganized the 'synagogue of Satan.'"

"But," said Brian, "was not Ham the father of the black race?"

"Oh, no!" said Samuel. "That is the usual modern idea, but it is not correct. In the Hebrew, Ham means 'burntess' or 'spiritual blackness,' but it has nothing to do with the colour."

"However, to continue. As I said, Nimrod refounded the

---

[1] Bristowe's "Sargon the Magnificent." [2] Gen. 4: 22.

'synagogue of Satan,' which within a few generations controlled Babylon, Egypt, and the other ancient civilizations."

"It was for this reason that Jehovah called Abraham to be the father of a race who would serve Him. Through the miraculous birth of Isaac[1], Jehovah commenced His new race, and through Isaac's son Jacob, whom He renamed Israel, He instituted the Israel nation, to whom you and I belong."

"At Mount Sinai, Jehovah gave Israel His Laws, promising great blessings if His Laws were kept, but on the other hand, great misfortunes if they were not kept, as in that case Israel would come under the control of Satan. He also promised that in the case of repeated disobedience, He would punish them for 'Seven Times'[2]. Now, according to ancient chronology, a 'Time' was 360 years, the 360 degrees of a circle, so that 'Seven Times' is 2520 years."

"As you know, Israel repeatedly failed to keep the Law, and were in consequence conquered by their enemies after each lapse, being freed by Jehovah whenever they repented and returned to the Law."

"As a result of Solomon's lapse into idolatry, into which he led the people, Israel was divided into the Southern Kingdom consisting of the Tribes of Judah and Benjamin, whilst the other Ten Tribes, under the leadership of the Tribe of Ephraim, became the Northern Kingdom. The latter lapsed into idolatry, and instituted the laws of Omri instead of the Law of the Lord, and after many warnings which went unheeded, apparently were given the promised 'Seven Times' punishment, as they have been 'lost' to their brethren of Judah ever since approximately 720 B.C. Isaiah tells us that Jehovah placed a judgement on them: 'Hear ye indeed, but understand not; and see ye indeed, but perceive not;' whilst Hosea states that Jehovah told him to tell Israel that He had divorced them, and that they were not His people, but that later He would again acknowledge them, and would again become a Husband to them. Many others of the prophets also state that Israel was to be blinded,

---

[1] Gen. 18: 11; 21: 1.   [2] Lev. 26: 16-46.

but all are unanimous that Israel is to become a world power under the kingship of Messiah. It would therefore appear that her blindness as to her identity, and her 'lost' condition is only to be during the 'Seven Times' punishment."

"But," said Brian, "surely if Israel's punishment started in 720 B.C. then her 'Seven Times' punishment will have already been completed."

"Just a minute," said his cousin. "You forget Judah, our own tribe. Judah also went into captivity for her idolatry, but not until about 120 years after Israel had done so. From that captivity, as you know, the main portion of Judah has never returned, and are 'lost.' It would appear that the blindness is to remain on both Israel and Judah until the punishment of the latter is also completed. At present the Jews are the only portion of the whole House of Israel who are not 'lost,' and the Sephardim are some of the descendants of Judah who are of Semitic blood."

"According to my calculations," he continued, "the punishment of Judah should be completed about the present time, and consequently there should be great events in the offing for both the 'lost' Judah and Israel in the very near future."

"However," he said, "I am afraid that you will consider this a long rigmarole, and not very much to the point, but I must lay the foundation in your mind for the facts on which my ideas are based, so we shall continue with the 'synagogue of Satan.' "

"That organization has always operated formerly from the capital of the empire holding world power. First, Babylon, where it was organized; later in Assyria. After the conquest of Assyria by Babylon, it returned to Babylon. After the destruction of Babylon it moved to Medeo-Persia; then to Greece under Alexander the Great; and thence to Rome, where it remained for many centuries, and whence its organization penetrated the western civilization. Until comparatively recently, it has directed its operations from Germany, probably

being responsible to a great extent for the latter's bid for
world power in 1914. After Germany's defeat in 1918, it
appears to have transferred its activities to Gog, where, as
you are aware, it has obtained control, for which control it had
been working for many years previously."

"As regards its activities, when it realized that the British
Empire was becoming a world power, and that Queen Victoria
attributed its growth and power to Bible-reading and to following Bible-teaching, the 'synagogue of Satan' immediately
began to invent infidel theories against the truth of the Scriptures, such as evolution, higher criticism, modernism, Communism, and other such theories. These theories they arranged
should be taught in the German universities and other seats of
learning as 'The New Learning,' and from there they in-
sinuated into the British universities, professors and teachers
of these theories, with a view to attacking Britain's greatness
at its source."

"If you study the matter," he continued, "you will find that
in each case the original exponent of each of these theories was
an apostate so-called German Jew, although some of these
theories were, after their introduction, taken up and elab-
orated by English and other Gentiles who had become their
exponents."

"Now it was Assyria, or Assur as she is called in the Hebrew,
that conquered and deported the Ten Tribes of Israel. Soon
afterwards Assyria was herself conquered and absorbed by
Babylon. The latter soon afterwards conquered and deported
Judah to Babylonia in two deportations. I might here add
that Assyria had some 75 years previously captured 46 of the
walled cities of Judah and had deported over 200,000 of their
inhabitants into Medeo-Persia, where the Ten Tribes had also
been deported. However, in each case the great majority of
the national records of both Judah and Israel disappeared.
In fact, nothing appears to have been left which might inform
future generations as to who their ancestors actually were."

"Even in the case of the some 40,000 Jews," he continued, "who returned to rebuild Jerusalem some 70 years after their captivity commenced, our Rabbis tell me that it was impossible to trace or discover many of their pre-captivity records."

"The 'synagogue of Satan' realize that Jehovah is to set up His world-wide kingdom through Messiah as king of both Judah and Israel, who are to be reunited. From my researches and from what our Rabbis have been able to discover, it is the 'synagogue of Satan' who are responsible for the loss of our former national documents and records, of which, no doubt, they still remain possessed. Hence they have been able to trace both Judah and Israel down the centuries, and know what present-day nations are their descendants. On the other hand, the present-day nations who are actually the descendants of Judah and Israel are quite unaware of that fact."

"In this way, it would appear that the 'synagogue of Satan' are trying to prevent Jehovah from setting up His kingdom under Messiah, as His people are unaware of Jehovah's intentions in regard to themselves. It was for this purpose, to prevent Jehovah's rule in the earth, that the 'synagogue of Satan' was organized. Humanly speaking, they appear to have been successful in their efforts. However, a study of the prophets shows that Jehovah will intervene when the 'Seven Times' are completed, will destroy the 'synagogue of Satan' and His other enemies, and through Messiah will set up His kingdom on earth for the Millenium."

"But," interjected Brian, "have you been able to discover what nations are Judah and Israel?"

"Yes," replied Samuel. "I am quite sure in my own mind on that point, as are several of our Sephardim Rabbis. It is too long a story to go into at present, so we shall have to leave it for a future meeting."

"I have now arrived," he continued, "at the point to which I have been working. So far as I have been able to discover, and as corroborated by many facts and also by some of my colleagues, the 'synagogue of Satan' works within the ranks of the Ashkenazim so-called Jews. I do not mean that all the Ashkenazim Jews are members of the society—far from it—but I do mean that the organization is controlled by certain of the Ashkenazim Jews, but by which ones I cannot yet tell, although there is little doubt as to who controls the International Finance end of it."

"However, Gog's attack is without doubt arranged by the 'synagogue of Satan' end of the Ashkenazim, and the object is to control Palestine.

"As you are aware, Palestine is the centre of the land surface of the earth. Those in control of Palestine, particularly if supplied with a preponderance of aircraft, can close the Suez Canal and thereby cut the lifeline of the British Empire, or if you prefer it, Commonwealth of Nations.

"The Ashkenazim, or perhaps I should say the 'synagogue of Satan' section of the Ashkenazim, have tried by every means to have Britain cede Palestine to them so that, when they had made the necessary arrangements with the nations whom they control, they might cut its lifeline and destroy the British Empire.

"By the way," he continued, "have you read the 'Protocols of the Learned Elders of Zion?'"

"No," replied Brian, "but I understood that they were a forgery."

"So the Zionists claim," Samuel said, "and they recently started a propaganda campaign to that effect, stating that over 20 times they had been proved in court to be a forgery, which is not true. What actually did occur was that in Geneva in 1933, the Zionists tried to get an order prohibiting the issue of the protocols, and called 16 witnesses, but the judge allowed the other side to call no witnesses. After many other such irregularities, the judge declared for them. However, the final ending was that on appeal by the other side, the Supreme Court dismissed the Zionists' case, and made them pay costs of 30,000 francs."

"Protocol No. 8 tells us, 'We must arm ourselves with all the weapons which our opponents might employ against us. We must search out in the very finest shades of expression and the knotty points of the lexicon of Law *justification* for those cases where we shall HAVE TO PRONOUNCE JUDGE-MENTS THAT MIGHT APPEAR ABNORMALLY AUDA-CIOUS AND UNJUST, for it is important that these resolutions should set forth in expressions THAT SHALL SEEM TO BE the most exalted moral principles cast into legal form.'"

"It must therefore be realized that in view of this statement, it makes little difference whether a Court pronounces the 'Protocols' to be a forgery or not, but we must instead examine them to see whether the agenda which they contain have or have not been carried out by world events since they were published in 1905; although the Meetings which they purport to represent are stated to have been held much earlier than that date."

"If world events have NOT followed the agenda laid down in the 'Protocols,' then they must undoubtedly be a forgery."

"On the other hand, if world events have followed the agenda laid down, then world events have themselves proved the 'Protocols' to be genuine and no forgery."

"Let us examine some of the agenda of a few of the first protocols, of which there are 24."

Taking a book from his desk, he opened it, and continued:

"Protocol No. 1 simply outlines in general the ideas of Zionism, whose countersign is stated to be 'Force and Make-believe.' It also states that they have already ruined the natural and genealogical aristocracy of the Goyim (Gentiles), and have raised on its ruins an aristocracy of their own educated classes, headed by the aristocracy of money, which statements you know to be true in Europe."

"The heading of Protocol No. 2, contains the following subjects of agenda: 'Economic Wars, the Foundation of Jewish (Zionist) Predominance. Figure-head Governments and

"Secret Advisers." Successes of Destructive Doctrines. Adaptibility in Politics. Part Played by the Press. Cost of Gold, and Jewish Sacrifice.' It is then stated that war must in future be on an economic basis, and that their international rights will then wipe out national rights; hence they will rule the nations. Have world events since then shown any signs of such a Plan?"

"To anyone who has studied the hold which International Finance has on the nations of the world," replied Brian, "there is no doubt that this plan has been most successful. The nations win the wars: International Finance wins the peace."

"Again," Samuel continued, "it is stated in the same protocol that they will through their controlled press, persuade the Gentiles to accept false theories as 'the dictates of science,' and arouse in them a blind confidence in such false theories so that they will not ask for (nor receive) any verification that such theories are actually true. They then continue, 'Do not suppose for a moment that these statements are empty words: think carefully of the successes we ARRANGED for Darwinism, Marxism, Nietzsche-ism. To us Jews at any rate, it should be plain to see what a disintegrating importance these directives have had upon the minds of the Goyim (Gentiles).'"

"Here is definite proof, provided that the protocols are not a forgery, that the Zionists originated Evolution, Communism, and Nazi-Socialism entirely for the purpose of leading the Gentile nations away from the truth. Now, since the date of the issue of the protocols in 1905, have the theories of Evolution, Communism, and Nazi-Socialism been drummed into the public mind by propaganda, particularly to the workers, and by lecturers, whom it is stated in Protocol No. 2, they will use as 'agentur,' meaning specialist agents? Further, have these theories been accepted by the public as 'the dictates of science,' but with no verification of their truth ever supplied?"

"Undoubtedly," Brian replied, 'Evolution has been accepted as a fact by the great majority of the public, including myself. As we know to our cost, Nazi-Socialism was accepted by Germany, whilst Italy accepted Fascism, which is another name for the same theories. Also Russia accepted Communism, as have so many of the other Continental nations recently."

"In that case," Samuel asked, "would you, from world events since its issue, consider Protocol No. 2 to be a forgery, or actually the outline of plans which have since been carried out successfully?"

"There appears to me to be no doubt that it was the outlining of a plan, which has since been put into effect," said Brian.

"Let us now take Protocol No. 3," continued Samuel, "in which it is stated that Zionism is the 'Symbolical Snake.' It is stated that the 300 'hidden heads' are the 'Head of the Snake.' The Protocol states that 'their goal is only a few steps off,' and that 'when the ring closes all the states of Europe will be locked in its coils.' "

"This protocol states that they have annihilated the aristocracy who were the only defence of the people, and who were inseparably bound up with the welfare of the people, and in consequence, 'the people have fallen into the grip of merciless money-grinding scoundrels who have laid a pitiless and cruel yoke upon the necks of the workers.' Again, in Protocol No. 6, it is stated that although the power of the aristocracy is dead, that their lands must be taken away from them, and that this can best be done by increasing taxes and particularly land taxes. Protocol No. 3 continues, 'We appear on the scene as the alleged saviours of the worker from this oppression when we propose to him to enter the ranks of OUR FIGHTING FORCES—Socialists, Anarchists, Communists. The aristocracy, who enjoyed by law the labour of the workers, were interested in seeing that the workers were well-fed, healthy, and strong. We are interested in just the OPPOSITE, in the diminution, the KILLING OUT of the Goyim (Gentiles.)' A few lines later on the protocol states, 'Hunger creates the right of Capital to rule the worker more surely than it was given to the aristocracy by the legal authority of kings.' It is then stated in this protocol that they will create a Universal Economic Crisis, whereby they will throw on the streets whole mobs of workers simultaneously in all countries of Europe. Now, have, or have not the statements of this protocol been fulfilled since 1905?"

"There is no doubt," Brian replied, "that all the nations of Europe have had the troubles enumerated in that protocol since the date of its issue; and although the same troubles have been to the fore in Britain and America, it would appear that they have been less successful in those countries. However, as regards the 'Universal Economic Crisis,' every civilized country in the world was affected by it from 1928 in Britain, and 1929 in America; whilst in every country in the world the great majority of the workers were thrown out of work, and suffered terrible want and hunger, especially in the Continental nations. Yes; I fear that there was a great 'diminution of the Goyim,' and particularly of the workers, as a result of that 'crisis,' now so well-known as the 'Great Depression.' "

"Do you then believe," Samuel asked, "that Protocol No. 3, issued in 1905, was a forgery, or that later world events have proved that it was a devilish plan?"

"Like many millions of others," Brian replied, "I remember too well the suffering of the world, and particularly of the poor, during that terrible depression to ever believe, if that protocol was published in 1905, that it is a forgery."

"In Protocol 4," Samuel continued, "it is stated: 'This is the reason why it is indispensable for us to undermine all faith, to tear out of the minds of the Goyim (Gentile) the very principle of Godhead and the spirit, and to put in its place arithmetical calculations and material needs.' "

"It is further stated in Protocol No. 4: 'In order to give the Goyim no time to think and take note, their minds must be directed towards industry and trade. Thus, all the nations will be swallowed up in the pursuit of gain, and, in the race for it, will not take note of their common foe'; whilst the next paragraph states that the result will be 'Their only guide is gain, that is, gold, which they will erect into a veritable cult, for the sake of those material delights which it can give.' "

"In Protocol No. 5 it is stated that: "The Holy unction of the Lord's anointed has fallen from the heads of kings in the eyes of the people, and WHEN WE ALSO ROBBED THEM OF THEIR FAITH IN GOD the might of power was flung upon the streets into the place of public ownership and WAS SEIZED BY US.' "

"Now, in general, have the agenda outlined in Protocols Nos. 4 and 5 been corroborated by world events since 1905?" Samuel asked.

"There can be little doubt that they have been," answered Brian. "The cult of gold and gain in the speculative markets just before the 'Universal Economic Crisis' would show also that the agenda have been most successfully carried out. Again I fear that the great majority of the people, particularly in Continental Europe, have little faith in God, but rather, trust in *pseudo* science and in material matters, and this attitude has been greatly developed in the last three decades."

"It is further stated in Protocol No. 9," Samuel continued. "We have fooled, bemused, and corrupted the youth of the Goyim in rearing them in principles and theories which are known to us to be false, although it is by us that they have been inculcated."

"This would account for our present juvenile delinquency," Samuel added, "that is, from having been taught false theories instead of the old truths. However, when youth is disillusioned as the result of Gog's attack and the failure of the false theories, this should create such a reaction that they will again seek the God of their fathers."

"Protocol No. 11 concludes: 'God has granted us, His chosen people, the gift of the DISPERSION, and in this which appears in all eyes to be our weakness, has come forth all our strength, which has now brought us to the threshold of sovereignty over all the world.' "

"Actually," said Samuel, "this is just the opposite of Jehovah's purpose in dispersing the 'Very Evil Figs, which cannot be eaten, they are so evil,' as He stated, 'and I will deliver them to be removed into all the kingdoms of the earth FOR THEIR HURT, to be a reproach and a proverb, a taunt and a CURSE, in all places whither I shall drive them.'[1] We therefore see that they are the 'Very Evil Figs' in the sight of Jehovah, and not His chosen people.

Again, Protocol 17 states: 'Freedom of conscience has been declared everywhere, so that now only years divide us from the moment of the complete wrecking of the Christian religion. As to other religions, we shall have still less difficulty in dealing with them.' "

Samuel added: "Hence we see that their main enmity is against Messiah and His Truth."

"Although we could go through the majority of the protocols with similar findings," Samuel continued, "we are wasting too much time, but I should like to point out that in Protocol No. 10 it is stated that they will exhaust the Gentiles by dissension, hatred, struggle, torture, by starvation, BY THE INOCULATION OF DISEASES. Remember that this was published in 1905 before inoculation for diseases had been introduced. Now, it is carried out in our armed services and in the schools. The public must be taught not to believe nor practice the false propaganda it reads in the press or hears over the radio, or we shall have even more sickness than we have had in recent years."

"However, I do want to read to you part of Protocol No. 9, as it explains a great deal and opens up new lines of thought. Protocol No. 9 states: 'Nowadays, if any states raise a protest

[1] Jer. 24: 9.

against us it is only *pro forma*, and AT OUR DISCRETION and by OUR DIRECTION, for their anti-Semitism is INDIS-PENSABLE TO US for the management of OUR LESSER BRETHREN. I will not enter into further explanations, for this matter has formed the subject of repeated discussions amongst us.' "

"Here we have a statement that the Zionists are the ones who DIRECT anti-Semitism against their 'lesser brethren.' As the Zionist leaders are in most cases Ashkenazim so-called Jews or other converts to Judaism, and as proved by ethnologists, not Semitic, it must be apparent that these attacks on the 'lesser brethren' referred to are attacks on the real Semitic Jews. It would appear that in this case both the voice and hands are those of Esau.[1]

"Now in Protocol No. 2, as already quoted to you, it is stated that they are responsible for Nietzsche-ism, which is Nazi-Socialism, and also Fascism. It would therefore appear that the Nazi and Fascist outbursts of anti-Semitism were directed by the Zionists against the real Semitic Jew."

"There were many rumours that Hitler was only a figure-head, and that he took his orders from the 'big interests' such as the 'I.G.' The statement in Protocol No. 9 as to who actually directs anti-Semitism would tend to prove that, in the cases of both Hitler and Mussolini, these rumours were correct."

"But that seems absurd," said Brian. "Why should Hitler attack Russia, the birthplace of the Ashkenazim so-called Jew, and which country is so greatly controlled by the Ashkenazim?"

"In view of the long range plans outlined in the protocols," Samuel said, "it might have been a deep-laid plan to have Germany's strength destroyed by Russia, so that Russia could absorb a defeated Germany; a further step towards world mastery. As you will remember, when Russia attacked Finland in 1939, her tanks and equipment were old and obsolete, and

---

[1] Gen. 27: 22.

she made a very poor showing against little Finland. I have often thought that this was an attempt to draw Hitler into an attack on Russia. If so, it was successful, and when the attack was made Russia had excellent equipment and very modern tanks and other armoured fighting vehicles."

"I know," Brian said. "I was beyond the Urals on 'a job' in 1934, and saw the Five Year Plan in operation."

"However," Samuel continued, "shortly, the Protocols outline the Zionist plans for world mastery by making the Gentiles lose their faith in God; then in their kings and hereditary leaders; to destroy the Gentile aristocracy by making heavy land and other taxes upon them, and then to have the so-called Jews who control the International Financial system take the places of the former aristocracy; by teaching the masses Socialism and Communism, to turn the workers against their former leaders and employers; to raise wages to a height which industry cannot pay, but at the same time to raise the prices of commodities to such a height that the workers are not benefited, but will instead be hungry, thus stirring up trouble between them and their employers. Whilst these things are taking place, they, who control International Finance, will remain outside the scene, being the 'hidden hand.' When the masses have revolted against these conditions, and have killed off their leaders and employers, the 'hidden hand' will through hunger and by other means 'rivet the chains on the masses once more.' "

"Except for their final world revolution by the masses, the plans outlined in the Protocols are shown by world events to have taken place exactly as outlined. It would appear that Gog's attack is now taking the place of the world revolution in their plans."

"As previously remarked, it is stated that the 300 'hidden leaders' are the 'Head of the Snake,' and in Protocol 3 it is stated, 'When the hour strikes for our Sovereign Lord of all the world to be crowned, it is these same hands which will sweep

away everything that might be a hindrance thereto.' This
would appear to be the reason for Gog's attack, as we are
told that he is to be crowned in Zion, which is at Jerusalem."

"Now the Snake represents the Serpent or Satan, so it would
appear that the 300 'hidden' members who form the 'Head of
the Snake' are actually the 'synagogue of Satan.'"

"Isaiah refers to Satan as thou 'which didst weaken the
nations,'[1] but from what we have seen of the plans outlined in
the protocols, it would appear that he had helpers in the
matter."

"Now that the British White Paper stopping Zionist immigration into the Holy Land is being put into effect they are
forced to make other plans, the undoubted result of which
is Gog's attack."

"However, their ultimate object is the destruction of the
British Empire, and then of the United States of America and
the other democratic nations by Gog and his allies, which
latter are all secretly or openly controlled by Ashkenazim
Jews, how many of which are members of the secret organization in question I am unable to say."

"You are therefore quite safe," he continued, "in quoting
me to your Chief as stating emphatically that Gog's attack is
the first stroke in a bid for undisputed world control by the
'synagogue of Satan,' and that if he will take my advice he
will put no trust whatever in any statements or promises made
by the Ashkenazim. You can give him the details of this conversation, and I have little doubt that he already has corrobor-
ative evidence to support my statements."

"Of course, both your Chief and you yourself realize," he
said, "that there are many so-called Jews who are converts to
Judaism only and, like the Ashkenazim, are not of Jewish
blood. They are neither Sephardim nor Ashkenazim, so it is
difficult to say on which side they will be. I know of many of
them who are members of the Zionist Party, and who will therefore probably follow the lead of that party."

---

[1] Isa. 14: 12.

Brian thanked him deeply both on behalf of his Chief and himself for his information and help in the matter, and asked when he could see him again in order to obtain his views as to what modern nations were the descendants of the former Judah and Israel nations.

Samuel replied that as it was a rather long story, it would be better if Brian came to dinner that evening, as they could then spend as long as was necessary on the subject.

Brian accepted gladly, provided that his Chief did not require his services and, after reiterating his thanks, left his cousin's office.

CHAPTER II.

"Lost" Israel Found.

Whilst Brian waited for a taxi, he bought a newspaper. The headlines were blazing forth Gog's attack, stating that his advanced troops had reached Hazor, but the main headline announced that His Majesty the King had appointed the following day to be a Day of Repentance and Intercession.

He soon arrived at his Chief's office, where he found that the latter could see him at once.

Brian reported his cousin's information in detail, his Chief nodding from time to time and occasionally asking a question.

When he had completed his report, his Chief said, "All this corroborates to a great extent reports which we have gathered during the last decade or more. I have repeatedly warned the government of what might be expected, but ever since the defeat of Hitler seemed to be assured, their whole policy has been one of 'Peace and Safety.'[1] Ostrich-like they have hidden their heads in the sands of self-deception, and have refused to face facts. It now looks as though any action they may take will be too late to save Palestine and the Suez."

After some further discussion of the situation, Brian's Chief said, "The 9th Army in Palestine has asked me to send someone to look into the activities of the Jewish population. As you are more conversant with that question than anyone else now available, I have decided to send you."

"A plane is leaving early tomorrow morning, so I shall arrange for your transportation by it to Jerusalem. I shall give you a letter of introduction to the G. O. C. 9th Army. Here is a copy of a report which their intelligence have sent me regarding the Jewish underground activities in that area. Study it carefully, and I think you will discover from the names involved that it is the Ashkenazim who are responsible for the subversive work."

After final directions as to co-operation with other agents

---
[1] I Thes. 5: 3.

operating in the area, and also some further information as
to the situation in Palestine, his Chief told Brian that he was
free until the morning, and bid him "Good-bye, and good
hunting."

Brian returned to his own office, where he phoned Samuel
that he would be on hand for dinner that evening, after which
he packed his attaché case, and returned to his rooms to pack
what kit was necessary.

That evening, Brian arrived punctually for dinner with his
cousin. The latter's wife was away visiting friends, so Samuel
was able to dismiss the butler between courses, and then turn
the conversation to the question of Judah and Israel.

He opened the subject by asking, "Do you know any of our
ancient pre-Captivity Hebrew language?" to which Brian
replied in the negative.

Samuel continued, "Before the Captivity, Israel used a form
of the Phoenician tongue and script. The word Phoenician, or
Phoenix as it was originally, is derived from Pa-Hanok, which
means House of Hanok; whilst Hanok is the Phoenician-Hebrew
for Enoch, who was the great grandfather of Noah."[1]

"On their return from the Babylonian Captivity, the Jews
used a corrupted language and script which displaced the
Phoenician of their ancestors. This fact, however, has led
modern historians to state that Israel were not conversant with
writing in Moses' day, as they have been unable naturally to
discover any records in post-Captivity Hebrew prior to about
500 B.C.; and appear to be ignorant of the fact that Israel
formerly used the Phoenician."

"Now, Israel were known to the other nations as Barat-
Phoenicians, which originally was B'r't-Phoenix, and B'r't,
later spelled Bryt or Brit, means 'Covenant.' Later, the
Phoenix or Phoenician was dropped, and they were called
'Barats' or 'Bryts.' "

"It might here be stated that later, in the Tel el Armarna
tablets whose date is given as about 1400 B.C., Dr. Langdon

---

[1] Gen. 5: 21-29, Haberman in "Tracing Our Ancestors."

states that Israel are referred to as Habiru or Abiri, being the ancient name for Hebrews."

"Similarly 'ish' or 'ishi' is the Phoenician-Hebrew for 'man,' or 'my man,' whilst 'ana' meant 'land' in the same ancient language."

"You and I live in a country called Brit-ain. This, in the ancient Phoenician-Hebrew, is the equivalent of 'Covenant Land.' Similarly, the people are called Brit-ish, or 'Covenant Man.' Also the Anglo-Saxons, when they invaded Britain, referred to the inhabitants as Britons, which in Hebrew meant 'Covenant Ones.' "

"Have you ever heard of any nation or people who are a Covenant people, other than Israel?"

"No," replied Brian, "but I have not given the matter any thought before."

"To bring out all the evidence in the matter," Samuel continued, "would make a long, long story, so I shall just give you a resumé of the facts and, if interested, shall give you the names of several books which thoroughly cover the matter, and which you can study for yourself."

"Jehovah told Abraham, 'In Isaac shall thy seed be called.'[1] In the ancient Phoenician-Hebrew, Isaac was spelled Tzk, which later changed to Sakh, Sak, or Sachs."

"Again, the prophet Amos refers to Israel as the House of Isaac."

"After the deportation of Ten-Tribed Israel into Medeo-Persia,[2] they were known as 'Sak-Geloth,' meaning 'prisoners of Isaac.' Later the 'Geloth' part of their name was dropped, and they were known as Saks or Saki, by which name they appear on various ancient eastern inscriptions, such as the Behistun Rock, whilst in other inscriptions they are shown as Beth-Sak, meaning House or people of Isaac."

"Later, a large number of them moved northwards across the Caucasus Mountains into Southern Russia, where they became known as Skuthai, being the Greek for the Median

[1] Gen. 21: 12. [2] II Kings 17: 6.

Sak-Geloth. Still later the Romans called them the Scythians, although all Scythians do not appear to have been Israelites."

"Many of the Saki remained in Media where, according to Professor Waddell, they became known as the Guti or Catti, derived from Gadil and meaning men of Gad or of Judah or both. Waddell further states that Catti is the word from which Scot is derived."

"It may interest you to note that from a cylinder bearing the name of Cyrus, King of Medeo-Persia, we learn that Gobryas, General of the Guti in Cyrus' army, took and destroyed Babylon in 536 B.C., thus commencing the fulfilment of Jeremiah's prophecy that Jehovah had appointed Israel as His Battle Axe and Weapons of War, with which He would break in pieces the heathen nations."[1]

"Daniel, in Chapter 5, tells us that Darius took Babylon, but 'Darius' means 'lord' or 'governor,' and is not a proper name, but a title. Hence this does not conflict with the statement on Cyrus' cylinder of record."

"Herodotus and Diodorus tell us that Cyrus was killed by the Massagetai when he tried to conquer them. Now Getai is the Medic form of Guti or Catti, the Phoenician-Hebrew name, and simply means 'wanderers.' whilst Massagetai means 'great wanderers' according to Professor Rawlinson."

"It was around 600 B.C.," continued Samuel, "that the Runic characters developed from the Phoenician script, and we find these Runic characters wherever the Saki, Getai, Massagetai, and later the Goths lived or migrated, across Russia, Northern Germany, Scandinavia, Scotland, Ireland, and also Iceland."

"The Sagas of the Saghs or Saks and Goths were written in Runic characters, and are considered today as being fictitious. Actually they hold the legendary lore of the heroes of ancient times, who were the forefathers of the Goths, the Skuthai or Scythians, the Getai or Catti, and the Saks of Sakland, south of the Caucasus."

[1] Jer. 51 : 20.

"In the region south of the Caspian Sea, where Israel disappeared, there the Angli and the Saxons appeared. Pliny tells us, 'The Sakai were among the most distinguished people of Scythia, who settled in Armenia, and were called Sacca-Sani.' Herodotus wrote, 'The Saki who were Skuths. . . . These Amyrgian Skuths are called Sakai.' He also writes that the Getai believed that after death they went to Zalmoxis, which means 'The God of Moses'; and that they named the country Moesia, for in it lived the 'people of Moses.'"

"Professor Chwolsen of Petrograd states that he has deciphered 700 tombstones in the Crimea, all of which state that they were set up to Israelites, and the dates are about 15 B.C."

"Ptolemy mentions 'a Scythian race, sprung from the Sakai, called Saxones,' whilst Albinus wrote, 'The Saxons were descended from the ancient Sacae of Asia, and that in process of time they came to be called Saxons.'"

"About 200 B.C. Odin's people, the Aesir, Asa, or Angli of Ariana east of the Caspian Sea, who were a branch of the Getai who had remained in Media for several centuries, drove the Sakai into Germany, where they appeared as Saxons."

"Now, our 'A' is derived from the Phoenician letter Aleph (bull) representing the horns of a bull, and referring to the time when the Autumn Equinox (Lunar) lay in Taurus the Bull, at which time Adam was created and the Adamic calendar commenced. Adam was given the birthright, which was represented by Aleph the Bull. Later, God gave the birthright to Abraham, Isaac, and Jacob, and the latter gave it to Joseph and Joseph's son Ephraim, whose tribal insignia was a bull."[1]

"Aesir, Asa, or Angli, therefore referred to Joseph the Birthright or Bull Tribe, as Ephraim and Manasseh represented the two horns of Taurus (or Aleph), but Ephraim had been given the Bull standard."

"In Phoenician-Hebrew, Ngl meant 'bull,' which later was changed to Angl or Engl. Angli would therefore refer to the Bull Tribe or Ephraim, and probably included Manasseh."

---

[1] Deut. 33: 17.

"About four centuries later, the Asa or Angli migrated to the Baltic and North Sea coasts, where they appeared as the Angles, and pushed their predecessors ahead of them into what are now the Scandinavian countries and Germany. Of Ephraim, Moses prophesied, 'His glory is like the firstling of his bullock, and his horns are like the horns of unicorns: with them he shall push the people together to the ends of the earth: and they are the ten thousands of Ephraim, and they are the thousands of Manasseh.' "[1]

"As you may read in any history of England, the Saxons, Angles, Danes, Vikings, and finally the Normans invaded England, and settled there."

"The Danes were known as the Tuatha de Danaan, meaning 'Tribe of Dan.' Dan were always a sea-faring people, and we are told in Judges, 'And why did Dan remain in ships?' From shortly after their arrival in the Promised Land, they kept emigrating into the Aegean Islands, whence they later moved northwestwards into Scandinavia and also Ireland, after first founding colonies in Iberia, now called Spain, which they named after their Hebrew name. A Jewish writer of the 9th Century A.D., Eldud by name, tells us, 'In Jereboam's time (990-970 B.C.) the Tribe of Dan, being unwilling to shed their brothers' blood, took a resolve to leave the country' (Palestine.)"

"As regards the Normans, Professor Hannay, in his 'European Race Origins,' demonstrates that they were the Tribe of Benjamin, which had been lent to Judah.[2] After their capture and deportation by Babylon, they became known as the Galatians of Asia Minor, the word being derived from 'Galutha,' the Babylonian name for 'prisoners.' Professor Hannay further demonstrates how these Benjamites left Galatia and Cappadocia, landing finally in Norway after many adventures, where they became known as the Vikings."

"In the 9th Century A.D. they invaded Northwestern France under Rolf the First, who became Duke of Normandy, and there

[1] Deut. 33: 17. [2] I Kings 11: 36; 12: 21.

accepted Christianity, and adopted the French language and customs. As you know, the Normans under William of Normandy, invaded England and defeated the Saxons at the Battle of Hastings, after which they conquered England."

"The Normans' insignia was a wolf, and this was the tribal insignia of Benjamin."[1]

"We can therefore see that Ten-Tribed Israel migrated into the British Isles by tribes, as prophesied by the prophet Isaiah,[2] and that the Angles changed the name to England after the Ephraim Tribal insignia of a bull or calf, the Hebrew for which was Ngl, Angl, or Engl."

"It is further evident that after their deportation into Media, Ephraim changed their name to Ngl-Tzksons, meaning Bull Tribe of Isaac, which later was altered by time and the introduction of vowels into Anglo-Saxons. In the Hebrew, Engl-ish would mean ' Bull-man,' which is probably the derivation of our John Bull."

"In the British Royal Coat-of-Arms, we still show the unicorn (or wild bull) of Ephraim, as referred to by Moses."

"Before the advent of the Anglo-Saxons, Danes, and other tribes, England was known as Brittam or Britain. Let us now see how it came by that name."

"After the destruction of Troy, Brutus, a Trojan prince, landed in Britain about 1103 B.C. and called the island 'Brytana,' or 'Covenant Land.'[3] Brutus, however, was a descendant of Zarah, a son of Judah, and he and his followers were of the Tribe of Judah."

"Brutus was Great Britain's original law-giver, introducing the Common Law that has been the foundation of British justice ever since. Lord Chief Justice Cope affirms: 'The original laws of this land were composed of such elements as Brutus first selected from the ancient Greek and Trojan institutions.' (Preface to Volume 3 of Report.)"

"Brutus' son, Albanact, conquered what is now Scotland, and called it Albania after himself. Professor Waddell states that

[1] Gen. 49: 29. [2] Isa. 41: 1. [3] British History Traced from Egypt and Palestine: "Phoenician Origin of Britons, Scots, and Anglo-Saxons"; "Ancient British Chronicles."

he has traced the history given in the 'Ancient British Chronicles,' both in the east and in the west, and that they are authentic, and have been corroborated by other authentic evidence. Waddell states further that they were always accepted as authentic in Britain until about 100 years ago, at which time the modern historians rejected them, he states, 'upon a kind of objection and mere dogmatic assertion, which, if applied to early Greek and Roman history, and to the Old Testament tradition, would equally entail their total rejection also. . . .' "

"We can therefore see that the 'synagogue of Satan' have been at work here also to keep the British from tracing their ancestors."

"Again, Professor Totten of Yale states that a Milesian prince, Gadelius or Gadil, and his followers landed in Uladh (now Ulster) in Northern Ireland about 700 B.C., and that Gadil was a descendant of Zarah, son of Judah, as were his followers. This is corroborated in the 'Chronicles of Erie,' written in Phoenician-Hebrew, and translated by Roger O'Connor. Further, Professor Waddell in his 'Phoenician Origin of Britons, Scots, and Anglo-Saxons,' states that 'Gadi' or 'Catti,' the former being the root of Gadil or Gadelius, is the origin of the word 'Scot.' "

"History shows that later some of these Scots, or followers of Gadil, migrated up the West Coast of Scotland, and after fighting with their relatives who had conquered Scotland under Albanact several hundred years earlier, settled amongst them."

"Still again, Haberman in 'Tracing Our Ancestors,' demonstrates that the descendants of the Pharez Branch of Judah, after their deportation into Babylonia and Medeo-Persia, escaped and migrated across Europe as the 'Yoti,' finally settling in what is now in English called Jutland, but which they named and still call Yahudaland. As you are probably aware, Yahuda is the Hebrew for Judah, whilst Yehudim is Hebrew for 'Remnant of Judah,' or Jews."

"From Yahudaland, as the Jutes, they invaded the East

Coast of Scotland about 500 A.D. where they settled amongst
their relatives, the Zarah-Judah Branch."

"I have in all cases checked the information quoted, as have
some of our Rabbis, and we are confident that they are sub-
stantially correct."

"Have you noticed that the insignia of Scotland is a Lion
Rampant? This, I have no doubt, is the ancient 'Lion of the
Tribe of Judah'[1], our tribal insignia, which later became the
insignia of the King of the House of David, and is to be that
of Messiah when He sets up His kingdom."

"Have you further noticed," he continued, "that the Zionist
Jews have taken as their insignia the 'Interlaced Triangles'
of Solomon, which the latter took after he had fallen into
idolatry, and had in consequence been warned by Jehovah that
the kingdom was to be rent from him, but in the days of his
son?"[2]

"It is interesting to note that Northern Ireland has taken
as its insignia the 'Harp of David,' the reason being that
Jeremiah the prophet brought to Ireland Tamar-Tephi, daughter of Zedekiah, King of Judah, when the latter was deported
to Babylon. There she married Eochaid, King of Ireland, of
the Zarah-Judah Branch. Irish tradition has it that Jeremiah
also brought with him the Harp of David, as well as the Lia
Phail, or 'Stone of Destiny,' which was later lent to Scotland
for the crowning of King Fergus in 498 A.D."

"The Lia-Phail or Lia-Fail remained in Scotland, and all
Scottish kings were crowned on it. Edward I brought it from
the Abbey of Scone in 1298 A.D. and placed it in Westminster
Abbey, as 'The Stone of Scone,' and on it all English or
British kings have since been crowned."

"I should advise you to read Rev. Allen's 'Judah's Sceptre
and Joseph's Birthright,' or Haberman's 'Tracing Our Ancestors' if you wish for definite historical evidence of these facts."

"Are there any questions you would like to ask, Brian, on
the facts which I have enumerated?"

[1] Gen. 49: 9.   [2] I Kings 11: 11.

"Yes, Samuel," Brian replied, "you have mentioned the Pharez and Zarah branches of Judah, but what about the Shelah Branch?"

"No one appears to have discovered any migrations of that branch into Britain or elsewhere. As you know, Shelah was the son of Judah by a Canaanite woman.[1] Abraham told Isaac not to marry a Canaanite, and was obeyed.[2] Isaac told his sons not to marry Canaanites. Jacob obeyed, but Esau married two Hittite women, Canaanites, which grieved Isaac and his wife.[3] Esau in consequence lost the birthright, as Jehovah told Rebecca that it was to be given to Jacob.[4] Our forefather Judah also sinned in marrying a Canaanite woman, by whom he had three sons, Er, Onan, and Shelah. Jehovah destroyed Er and Onan, without issue, as 'they displeased Him,' but allowed Shelah to live."[5]

"However, Jeremiah informs us in his 24th chapter that Jehovah told him that He had divided Judah into 'Very Good Figs' and 'Very Evil Figs'; that He had already sent the 'Good Figs' out of the land 'for their good,' as they would eventually serve Him whole-heartedly. On the other hand, the 'Very Evil Figs' were to be dispersed throughout all the kingdoms of the earth, and to be a 'reproach and a proverb, a taunt and a curse' wherever they were; also that the 'Evil Figs' were Zedekiah and his princes, and those who remained in Jerusalem and in the land, and also in the land of Egypt, where some had fled."

"Now, the majority of Judah had been deported prior to the prophecy of Jeremiah, and these were the Pharez and Zarah branches, whilst those who were with Zedekiah in the final deportation had, according to Josephus the historian of Judah, the earmarks of the Shelah Branch."

"It would further appear from the records of the Jews who returned to rebuild Jerusalem after the Babylonian Captivity, that the majority of them were Shelanites, although a certain proportion were of the Pharez line, and some even of the House of David, who belonged to the Pharez line. In A.D. 70, the

---

[1] Gen. 38: 1-10. [2] Gen. 24: 3. [3] Gen. 26: 34; 28: 1. [4] Gen. 25: 23. [5] Gen. 38: 1-10.

Jews were dispersed 'into all the kingdoms of the earth,' as prophesied by Jeremiah, so from the fulfilment, it would appear that the Jews must have been the 'Evil Figs' portion of Judah."

"To relieve your mind, I may say that the family to which we both belong was of the Pharez line, and never returned to Judea after the Babylonian Captivity. Our ancestors were in the first deportation into Medeo-Persia, whence they migrated to Gades, now called Cadiz in Spain, and where they remained for many centuries. I have checked this information carefully, and have had it substantiated from two sources. On the other hand, our family records show that we sent representatives to the Passover at Jerusalem every fifth year, and so kept up our national worship at its source."

"As our ancestors were deported prior to the date of Jeremiah's prophecy, which Ussher places at 600 B.C. and were not with Zedekiah and those remaining with him, it would appear that we are not classified as 'Evil Figs' in Jehovah's books."

Samuel paused, and Brian interjected, "You have stated that Northern Ireland was populated by Zarah-Judah. What about Southern Ireland?"

"Southern Ireland," replied his cousin, "was populated originally by descendants of Ham, not Shem, according to 'Chronicles of Erie' and other ancient genealogical records. They would therefore be partially of Canaanitish origin through Naamah, Ham's wife. Haberman states that they were Canaanites, which would account for our troubles in Southern Ireland."

"Later the Tuatha de Danaan, which is the Hebrew for Tribe of Dan, arrived in Southern Ireland, but there were continual wars between them and the Hamitic inhabitants, so that finally they made a treaty with Zarah-Judah in Northern Ireland, and Eochaid of Zarah-Judah became Heremon, or Head King of Ireland, and between them they kept the Hamitic people in subjection. The latter are the 'Black Irish.' As you will remember, it was Eochaid who married Tamar-Tephi,

Zedekiah's daughter, which reunited the Pharez and Zarah Royal Houses."

"However, to return to Britain, on the arrival of the Angles in Britain about 450 to 550 A.D.," he continued, "they, as Ephraim and Manasseh, 'pushed the people together' as prophesied by Moses, and the Britons of Zarah-Judah were pushed into Wales, Devon, and Cornwall. The Welsh still call themselves 'Bryth-Y-Brithan,' meaning 'Covenanters of the Land of the Covenant,' which is derived from the ancient Welsh Triads."

"It might further be said that the Bretons of Brittany in France are of the same stock as the Welsh. So similar is their language that even today Welsh and Bretons can converse together, each using his own tongue."

"The Royal Coat-of-Arms of our British King carry the Lion of the Tribe of Judah, the Unicorn, or bull, of Ephraim, and the Harp of David, thus showing that the prayer of Moses, 'Hear, Jehovah, the voice of Judah, and bring him to his people,'[1] has been answered, and also that the prophecy of Ezekiel, 'And I will make them one nation in the land upon the mountains of Israel, and one King shall be King to them all: and they shall no more be two nations, neither shall they be divided into two kingdoms any more at all,' has long since been fulfilled.[2] In prophecy 'mountains' means 'kingdoms.' "

"As regards the British Throne, Queen Victoria decided to have a chart of her genealogy made up, so accordingly commissioned separately three genealogists to work out the chart in question, each one being unaware that any other genealogist was similarly engaged. When the first genealogist presented his chart, it showed that Queen Victoria was descended directly from King David of Israel. The story states that the Queen was most indignant, saying that she was a Gentile and not a Jewess, and would have nothing to do with the chart. Then the second genealogist, and finally the third, presented their

---

[1] Deut. 33 : 7.   [2] Ezek. 37 : 22.

charts, each showing that the Queen was descended from King David, although different in minor details."

"The Queen then studied the question, and finally took pride in the matter when she saw that David's Line had been promised the Israel Throne forever by Jehovah.[1] Now the chart hangs in a prominent place, and our later kings have since been proud of their Davidic descent."

"If you would like to study the question further, I can recommend, 'The Royal House of Britain,' by Rev. W. H. Milner, which gives conclusive evidence of the facts."

"It seems that Israel, as represented by the British Commonwealth of Nations and the United States of America, which has the Tribal Insignia and Heraldry of Manasseh, the Thirteenth Tribe of Israel, have become 'Chief of the Nations,' as prophesied.[2] However, if you would like to study the matter further, I advise you to read, 'European Race Origins,' by Professor H. B. Hannay: 'God's Great Plan,' by R. L. Williams; 'Phoenician Origin of Britons, Scots, and Anglo-Saxons,' by Professor Waddell; also the 'Ancient British Chronicles,' and 'Chronicles of Erie.' An excellent book, written by an American, F. Haberman, is 'Tracing Our Ancestors,' as the author takes us from the creation of Adam to the present day, quoting for his facts authorities both ancient and modern whose writings are considered authoritative in their various subjects."

"However, as we have long since finished dinner, let us go into my study, where I have books and documents handy to prove my points should you not have been entirely satisfied with my explanations, or if I have not made myself clear on any point."

---

[1] II Sam. 7: 16.   [2] Jer. 31: 7; Amos 6: 1.

CHAPTER III.

A Jew Finds His Messiah.

They moved into Samuel's study, where cigars were lighted whilst the butler brought in decanters and glasses. After pouring drinks for themselves and sitting down, Samuel said, "Of course I have given you only a short resumé of the stories of Judah's and Israel's migrations into the 'Appointed Place' promised by Jehovah to David,[1] but have I made the matter clear, or are there any points which you question?"

"Knowing your habit of never taking anything for granted," Brian replied, "and the fact that you never jump at conclusions, I am sure that you have studied the matter fully and have had conclusive evidence, as otherwise you would not have accepted it. If therefore you have accepted it as proved, from what you have told me, so shall I."

"Thank you for your confidence," Samuel replied, "but when you have time, do read some of the books which I have recommended, as it is most interesting to study the history of our race, and to compare that history with the prophecies of our ancient prophets, which have so wonderfully been fulfilled in every detail up to the present time. That study has changed my whole outlook on life, so if you are not bored, I shall give you a short outline of what I mean."

Brian having dutifully replied that he was not at all bored and would be really interested in Samuel's further conclusions, his cousin continued, "Prior to finding 'lost' Israel and Judah, I had held the modern view that the Scriptures were more or less legendary and had little to do with the present day. The Promised Messiah had not come to set up His Israel kingdom on a world-wide basis, but instead Israel and the main part of Judah were 'lost,' whilst the Jews were dispersed and not a nation at all, nor had they been a nation since the destruction of Jerusalem in A.D. 70. For hundreds of years, our Rabbis had prayed each Sabbath in the synagogues for our lost

[1] II Sam. 7: 10.

brethren of Israel and Judah, in which prayers the congregation joined, but apparently Jehovah had paid no attention to
our prayers, and Israel were apparently dispersed amongst
the Gentiles, as prophesied by Amos, Hosea, and other prophets.
The Scriptures therefore appeared to me to have little basis
of truth in them, and I considered that the prophets had been
mistaken in thinking that Jehovah had made the statements
which they attributed to Him."

"The finding of Israel and Judah, so wonderfully preserved
and now 'Chief of the Nations' as prophesied[1] changed my viewpoint at once, and I began to study the Scriptures, and particularly the prophecies, with a new light and interest."

"As a result of my studies of the prophets, I discovered what
our religious leaders had apparently overlooked or misunder-
stood. That is that Messiah appeared to have two roles, one
as King of Israel, whilst He was also referred to in Isaiah and
other prophets as 'Redeemer of Israel,'[2] and as 'brought as a
Lamb to the slaughter,' and also to be 'wounded for our
transgressions' and 'with His stripes we are healed.' "[3]

"There were so many such statements throughout the
prophets that at first I was greatly puzzled."

"One day when in a bookseller's I saw a small pamphlet
entitled 'Inspiration of the Scriptures Scientifically Demonstrated.' I bought a copy, which I read that evening. In it
the author claimed that the Scriptures of what are called the
Old and New Testaments, or Covenants, had a structure in
their texts of sevens and multiples of sevens, that is in the
original Hebrew and Greek."

"I accordingly made this test in a copy of the Hebrew Scriptures which I had, but could find no trace of the structure of
sevens. Fortunately I again read the pamphlet, and discovered
that the author, a scientist named Panin, had stated that it
was the *vocabulary* only of the original Hebrew and Greek
Scriptures which answered to the test, and not the Scriptures
as written out fully by the scribes, or monks in the case of the

---

[1] Jer. 31: 7; Amos 6: 1.   [2] Isa. Chap. 53.   [3] Isa. Chap. 53.

New Testament, and with many words interpolated into the text by the writers."

"I then obtained a copy of the original Hebrew Scriptures from one of our Rabbis for the purpose of making the test, and was very much surprised and interested to find that the author's claims were fully substantiated. As the Hebrew Scriptures were written over a period from about 1490 B.C. to 397 B.C., or practically 1100 years, and as all contained this structure of sevens, which Panin named 'numerics,' it was apparent that One Mind must have inspired all the writers as to each word written."

"As Panin stated that the same 'numeric' structure was contained throughout the New Testament also, I borrowed a copy of these writings in the original Greek and Aramic, and made the same test with them. To my astonishment they also contained the same structure of sevens, so it was conclusive that the same Mind must also have inspired the New Testament, and that it also must be authentic. At first I tried to avoid this conclusion, but had to admit that it must be true."

Samuel paused, and Brian interposed, "Exactly what was the test to which you refer, as I am not at all clear on the point?"

"Sorry," his cousin replied. "In the Hebrew, in which the Old Testament is written, and in the Greek, in which the New Testament is written, the letters of the alphabet are used as numbers, certain of the letters having numerical significances. In place of the letters of the alphabet, Panin transposed the numeral significances, and as a result discovered that each complete phrase of the Bible was made up of sevens and multiples of seven, which number appears to be the number of the divine cycle. These 'numerics' Ivan Panin demonstrated in his book 'Bible Numerics,' much more fully than he did in his small pamphlet."

"I shall now read you an extract from Panin's 'Inspiration of the Scriptures Scientifically Demonstrated,' which will explain the test more clearly than I could do." Taking a pamphlet from his desk, he read the following extract,

" 'The first 17 verses of the New Testament contain the genealogy of the Christ. It consists of two main parts; Verses 1-11 cover the period from Abraham, the father of the chosen people, to the Captivity, when they ceased as an independent people. Verses 12-17 cover the period from the Captivity to the promised Deliverer, the Christ."

" 'Let us examine the first part of this genealogy."

" 'Its vocabulary has 49 words, 7 x 7. This number is itself seven (Feature 1) sevens (Feature 2), and the sum of its factors is 2 sevens (Feature 3). Of these 49 words 28, or 4 times seven, begin with a vowel; and 21, or 3 sevens, begin with a consonant (Feature 4)."

" 'Again; these 49 words of the vocabulary have 266 letters, or 7 x 2 x 19; this number is itself 38 sevens (Feature 5), and the sum of its factors is 28, or 4 sevens (Feature 6), while the sum of its figures is 14, or 2 sevens (Feature 7). Of these 266 letters, moreover, 140, or 20 sevens, are vowels, and 126, or 18 sevens, are consonants" (Feature 8).

" 'That is to say: Just as the numbers of words in the vocabulary is a multiple of seven, so is the number of its letters a multiple of seven: Just as the sum of the factors of the number of the words is a multiple of seven, so is the sum of the factors of the number of their letters a multiple of seven. And just as the numbers of words is divided between vowel words and consonant words by sevens, so is their number of letters divided between vowels and consonants by sevens."

" 'Again; of these 49 words 35, or 5 sevens, occur more than once in the passage; and 14, or 2 sevens, occur but once (Feature 9); seven occur in more than one form, and 42, or 6 sevens, occur in only one form (Feature 10). And among the parts of speech the 49 words are thus divided: 42, or 6 sevens, are nouns; seven are not nouns (Feature 11). Of the nouns 35, or 5 sevens, are proper names, seven are common

nouns (Feature 12). Of the proper names 28 are male ancestors of the Christ, and seven are not (Feature 13)."

"Panin gives further features, but this should be sufficient
to show the structure of the numerics.'"

"As regards the structure of the 'numerics' in the Old Testament, Panin states:

" 'There remains only to be added that by precisely the same
kind of evidence the Hebrew Old Testament is proved to be
equally inspired. Thus the very first verse of Genesis has seven
words, 28 letters, or 4 sevens: to name only two out of the
dozens of numeric features of this one verse of only seven
words.'"

Samuel put away the pamphlet and continued, "I have spent
many, many hours in testing these numerics, and have found
that the vocabularies of the originals, when the *interpolated
words* are omitted, fully substantiate Panin's claims for them."

"As a result, it was apparent that the claims of the New
Testament, or New Covenant, that Jesus was Messiah must
be true. I always refer to Him now as Messiah, which is the
Hebrew for the Greek word Christ, meaning 'Anointed.' Similarly Jesus, which means 'God Our Saviour,' is the Romanized
version of Je-Hoshua, or Joshua, meaning Jehovah-Saviour,
which is His Hebrew Name, as it was the Roman Church which
took the Romanized version of His name."

"As you are probably aware," Samuel continued, "in the
Bible, from the time when God revealed His Name of Jehovah
to Moses as His Covenant Name to Israel,[1] that Name is used
throughout in the original Hebrew when in connection with
Israel. His Name of Jehovah, with or without its compounds,
is used in connection with His Redemptive characteristics to His
Covenant People Israel. On the other hand, His Name of
Elyon El, meaning the 'Most High God' is used by and in
connection with Gentiles."

"The translators, taking the Gentile viewpoint, have
throughout translated 'Jehovah' as 'Lord,' or in His compound

---

[1] Exod. 3: 14.

Name, 'Jehovah Elohim,' as 'Lord God.' He also refers to Himself in His Redemptive capacity by seven other compound Names, such as 'Jehovah-Tsidkenu,' The Lord Our Righteousness' and also 'Jehova-Rapha,' 'The Lord that Healeth Thee,' sometimes written 'Jehovah-Ropheka.' "

"The discovery that Joshua or Jesus was Messiah caused a complete revolution of my ideas. My first reaction was to go to the Rabbis and explain the matter, but I decided that first I should study it more carefully in order to be able to explain where and why our ancestors had gone astray."

"A study of the sin-offerings in Leviticus[1] showed that from the Hebrew word there used, the sacrifices only 'covered' the sins, but did not do away with them."

"On the other hand, the New Testament is the New Covenant promised in Jeremiah[2] and other prophets, where Jehovah said that He would write His laws in our hearts. This is the theme of the New Covenant Scriptures, particularly the epistles of Paul, especially Hebrews, where he explains fully that the 'covering over' of sins by animal sacrifices was only until the Righteousness of God appeared through the sacrifice of His Son, which sacrifice made an end of sins.[3]

"This had been prophesied by Daniel about 538 B.C. as he was told by the angel Gabriel, 'Seventy weeks are determined upon thy people and upon thy Holy City, to Finish the Transgression, and to Make an End of sins, and to make Reconciliation for Iniquity, and to bring in Everlasting Righteousness, and to seal up the vision and prophecy, and to anoint the Most Holy.'[4] Here we have a prophecy which sets out fully the purpose of Messiah's First Advent. Similarly Isaiah tells us Who He is, stating, 'For unto us a Child is born, unto us a Son is given; and the government shall be upon His shoulder: His Name shall be called Wonderful, Counsellor, the Mighty God, the Everlasting Father, the Prince of Peace.'[5] Which shows what His role in both His First and Second Advents was to be."

"On looking into the matter and studying Daniel's writings,

---

[1] Lev. 16: 5-6. [2] Jer. 31: 33. [3] Heb. 1: 3. [4] Dan. 9: 24. [5] Isa. 9: 6.

I found that Messiah had been born at the time prophesied in Daniel's ninth chapter, and that our Jewish leaders had correctly figured the time stated in the prophecy, and were expecting Messiah to come at the time at which He did, but they expected Him to come as King in power, absolutely ignoring the prophetical statements in Isaiah and the other prophets that He was to come as Redeemer of Israel and Judah."

"As they very well knew, both Israel and the main part of Judah had failed to keep the Law of the Lord, and had been divorced as told us in Hosea,[1] and it was therefore necessary for the Kinsman-Redeemer to redeem His people from the penalty of death due them under the Law, and to carry out the Law as regards the Kinsmen-Redeemer Himself paying the penalty in full."[2]

"Messiah has therefore by His sacrifice redeemed us from the Law, and placed us again under the Abrahamic Covenant, given as the result of faith on the part of Abraham and which we, his descendants, must accept by faith and not by works. This is where the Jewish Ecclesiastics went astray."

"As you will remember, Messiah was to be a stumbling-stone to many,[3] which would appear to be the Pharisees of His day on earth, and also to the present day Pharisees. I refer to those self-righteous people of both then and now who are so satisfied with their own righteousness, that they refuse, perhaps unconsciously and unknown to themselves, to really accept His Righteousness in their hearts."

"I have expounded these facts, quoting the prophets and other Scriptures, to several of our Rabbis, and am glad to say that three of them are inclined to accept them, and are trying to expound them to the other Sephardim Rabbis. The Ashkenazim, however, will not listen to them, nor show any interest, as their attitude to Israel is that prophesied in Ezekiel,[4] which states, 'Get you far from the Lord: unto us is this Land given in possession;' whilst actually they have no right to the Land on any grounds."

[1] Hos. 1: 9; 2: 2.   [2] Lev. 25: 48.   [3] Isa. 8: 14; Rom. 9: 33.   [4] Ezek. 11: 15.

"However, at Messiah's first advent, the Jewish religious leaders were quite satisfied with their own righteousness, and were not a bit interested in this role of Messiah, but wished Him to come as King to free them from Rome and set up His world-wide kingdom under Israel. They therefore rejected Him and, so that the people would not accept Him, forced the Romans to crucify Him."

"Afterwards, when such proof of His resurrection was forthcoming that they could not refute it, and as Daniel had so clearly prophesied the date of His coming that they saw that they had had every ground on which to accept Him, they then stated that Daniel's prophecies were heretical, and removed his writings from their Scriptures, so that the people would not discover what they had done."

"You then consider," said Brian, "that the Jewish religious leaders' purpose in having the Messiah crucified was so that they could retain their rulership of the Jews."

"Yes," Samuel replied, "but only part of them took that attitude, as many of the priests and rulers had accepted Him as Messiah, as had many of the people. A certain section of them only worked to destroy Him, as we are told that the chief priests and elders of the people took counsel that they might by subtilty take Him and kill Him, for they feared the people, who considered Him to be a prophet.[1] We are given a hint in the records of those returning from Babylon to rebuild Jerusalem as to who they were who continually opposed Him, as it is stated, 'The children of Adonikam, six hundred, sixty, and six.'[2] Here we have the anti-Christ number 666,[3] which is also supposed to be the secret sign of the 'synagogue of Satan,' whilst 'Adonikam' in the Hebrew means 'Lord of the enemy.' "[4]

"It would therefore appear that Adonikam's descendants were members of the 'synagogue of Satan,' and that in the five centuries which elapsed between the rebuilding of Jerusalem and Messiah's first advent, they had seized the power in Jeru-

---

[1] Matt. 26: 4.   [2] Ezra 2: 13.   [3] Rev. 13: 18.   [4] Bullinger's Bible, Pt. 1.

salem, which is borne out by certain facts. King Herod and his followers were Idumeans, a Turko-Mongol breed, as are the Ashkenazim so-called Jews, whom I consider to be related to the Herodians. Now, we are told that the Pharisees took counsel with the Herodians as to how they might destroy Messiah,[1] so that it would appear that the descendants of Adonikam and the Herodians worked together."

"Further, it should not be forgotten that Messiah Himself said to those Jews who continually opposed Him, 'Ye are of your father the devil, and the lusts of your father ye will do. He was a murderer from the beginning, and abode not in the truth, because there is no truth in him.[2] As Adonikam means 'Lord of the enemy,' it seems apparent that He was speaking to his descendants."

"Again, He said to those same Jews, 'Ye believe NOT, because ye are NOT of My sheep.'[3] Now in the Scriptures, Israel alone are referred to as 'sheep': hence Messiah's remarks meant that the Jews in question were not of Israel, and if not of Israel, then they could not be of Judah, but must have been of foreign blood masquerading as Jews."

"But surely Jesus Himself was a Jew," said Brian.

"Absolutely not," replied Samuel. "We are told in the genealogy of His mother Mary in Luke that she was a descendant of David, and David was given a separate House of his own.[4] The genealogy in Luke 3, appears to be that of Joseph, as the translators have translated that he was the son of Heli, whilst actually he was the son-in-law, as Heli was the father of Mary. This was in accordance with the Jewish usage of calling a son-in-law a son. Joseph's genealogy is given in Matthew 1; Mary's in Luke 3."

"Again, Messiah is referred to as 'Son of David' in many places in the Gospels, whilst in His triumphal entry into Jerusalem, the people acclaimed Him as 'Son of David.'[5] No: He was no Jew, but of the House of David."

"Do not forget that neither you nor I are Jews in the strict

[1] Mark 3: 6. [2] John 8: 44. [3] John 10: 26. [4] II Sam. 7: 16. [5] Matt. 21: 9.

sense of the term, and there are undoubtedly many other Semitic or Sephardim so-called Jews who are in the same category as ourselves. Our ancestors were deported in the first deportation, and were of the Pharez branch, whilst the Jews are the descendants of those who were deported with King Zedekiah in the final deportation.[1] Again, do not forget that it was the King of Babylon who appointed Zedekiah as King of Judah, changing his name from Mattaniah to Zedekiah,[2] and that Zedekiah was not of the ruling line by direct descent."

"Then what did Jesus mean when He said that salvation was of the Jews?"[3] Brian questioned.

"He was speaking from the viewpoint of Daniel's prophecy, which states: 'Seventy weeks (490 years) are determined upon thy people and upon thy Holy City, to finish the Transgression, and to make an End of sins, and to make Reconciliation for iniquity, and to bring in Everlasting Righteousness, and to seal up the vision and prophecy, and to anoint the Most Holy.'[4] The Jews crucified Messiah, Who offered Himself freely,[5] and thus by their act brought in Everlasting Righteousness, or Salvation, for all who accepted Him as their Saviour. As regards the 'sealing of the vision and prophecy,' the Jews have done this by stating that they are the Chosen People, whereas it is Israel and the 'Good Figs' of Judah who are the Chosen People. Actually it is the Ashkenazim so-called Jews who have adopted this attitude more than have the true Semitic Jews, but in any case it has had the effect of leading the ecclesiastics away from looking for the real Israel and Judah, thus fulfilling that part of the prophecy also."

"At least you must admit that the Apostles were Jews," said Brian.

"Only one of them was a Jew," Samuel replied. "That was Judas Iscariot."

"All the others were Galileans,[6] who were of the Tribe of Benjamin, as was St. Paul.[7] Messiah Himself is referred to many times in the Gospels as Jesus of Nazareth, and Nazareth

---

[1] Jer. 24: 9. [2] II Kings 24: 17. [3] John 4: 22. [4] Dan. 9: 24. [5] John 10: 18. [6] Acts 1: 11; 2: 7. [7] Romans 11: 1.

was in Galilee. It was in Galilee that He spent most of His time and ministry, going up to Jerusalem only for the Passovers and other feasts, as when He came into Judea the Pharisees and Elders tried to kill Him."

"Moses prophesied of the Tribe of Benjamin, 'The Beloved of Jehovah (Messiah) shall dwell in safety by him (Benjamin) and Jehovah shall cover Him all the day long, and He shall dwell between His shoulders.' "[1]

"You may remember," Samuel continued, "that when Jehovah rent the Kingdom of Israel from Solomon's son, Rehoboam, leaving him one tribe only,[2] that He gave him the Tribe of Benjamin, saying, 'that David My servant may have a light always before Me in Jerusalem, the city which I have chosen Me to put My Name there.' "[3]

"After the return from the Babylonian Captivity, some of Benjamin returned, but they settled in Galilee in the northern part of the Holy Land, whilst the Jews settled in Judea and Jerusalem, in the southern part."

"Well, Samuel," Brian said, "I have caught you out this time. You say that all the Apostles except Judas Iscariot were Galileans. What about Simon, whom we are told was a Canaanite?"[4]

"You are quoting from the Authorized Version of the Latin Septuagint," Samuel replied. "The Revised Version, as well as the other modern translations, such as Weymouth's and Panin's Numeric Translations, in which the numeric test is made throughout to ensure that the correct word is used, and that it follows the 'numeric' pattern of the Scriptures, have all corrected this mistranslation. It should read, 'Simon the Canaanean:' that is from Cana of Galilee, where Messiah performed His miracle of making wine.[5] Thus you see that Simon was also a Galilean and not a Canaanite. Does that satisfy you?"

"Quite," Brian said. "I see that one must be very careful

---

[1] Deut. 33: 12.   [2] I Kings 11: 13.   [3] I Kings 11: 36.   [4] Matt. 10: 4; Mark 3: 18.
[5] John 2: 3-10.

to check the translations, as the translators appear to have made many errors."

"Sometimes intentionally, I fear," Samuel replied. "Remember that Haberman demonstrates that the Latin race are the descendants of the Canaanites, and their church would very much like to be able to point to one of the Apostles as being a Canaanite."

"However, you may remember that Messiah said of Judas that he was a devil,[1] so it is possible that he was secretly a member of the 'synagogue of Satan.' As you know, Judas finally repented,[2] which I think may be symbolical that the Semitic Jews will also repent, and accept Messiah after the destruction of Gog, and before His return, as Jehovah said, 'For I will cleanse their blood, that I have NOT cleansed:'[3] and their blood can only be cleansed by accepting the blood of Messiah for its cleansing."

"It seems to me a peculiar thing," Brian said, "that in view of all the actions taken against Jehovah and His Word by the 'synagogue of Satan,' that that organization is not mentioned in the Scriptures."

"Oh, but it is!" replied Samuel. "Messiah Himself tells us of it. In Revelation 3: 9, He states, 'Behold, I will make them of the synagogue of Satan, which say they are Jews, and are NOT, but do lie, behold I will make them to come and worship before thy feet, . . . etc.'"

"Here Messiah is speaking to those who have kept His Word, and have not denied His Name; the Romanized version, 'Jesus,' meaning 'God Our Saviour.' According to the Scofield Reference Bible, this refers to the 'True Church' within the professing church; that is those who believe in God's Word and accept God's Righteousness through the sacrifice of Messiah, as opposed to those who believe in the church and works for salvation."

"This latter is the teaching of the Modernists and Higher Critics, who have been led astray by the theories of the 'syna-

---

[1] John 6: 70. [2] Matt. 27: 3-5 [3] Joel 3: 21.

gogue of Satan' through 'scholarship,' and no longer believe in God's Word as being inspired, nor in the Divinity of Messiah but, like the Jewish religious leaders of His day, believe in their religious system and in works, and consider that their righteousness is such that they need no Redeemer and Saviour."

"This is the Great Apostasy prophesied by Paul, Peter, Jude, and even by Messiah Himself. In fact St. Paul tells us that the Day of Christ will not come except there come first a 'falling away,'[1] and the Greek word used for 'falling away' is apostasy; that is departing from divinely revealed truth."

"We can therefore see the justice of this judgment which will make the 'synagogue of Satan,' on account of their activities which caused this Great Apostasy, worship at the feet of those who, in spite of those activities, have still believed in the truth of God's Word, and kept faith in the name of Jesus, as 'God Our Saviour.' "

"At the present time," Samuel continued, "the Zionists have put on a campaign amongst the Modernist ecclesiastics to have any reference to the guilt of the Jewish religious leaders for the Crucifixion of Messiah expunged from the Bible. As Messiah said to those leaders who continually opposed Him, and of whom the present day Zionist leaders appear to be the spiritual descendants, 'Ye are of your father the devil, and the lusts of your father ye will do. He was a murderer from the beginning, and abode not in the truth, because there is no truth in him.' "[2]

"From their attitude, the present day Zionist leaders are also afraid of the truth, and prefer lies. Their spiritual ancestors said to Pilate when the latter tried to save Messiah, 'His Blood be on us, and on our children:'[3] and His Blood will still be upon them whether they expunge the references to the guilt of their forefathers from the Bible or not."

"There is only one way in which they can have the guilt of His Blood removed. That is by accepting Him as their Saviour, Redeemer, and Messiah; as He is the Way, the Truth, and

---

[1] II Thes. 2: 3. [2] John 8: 44. [3] Matt. 27: 25.

the Life;[1] and, as He said, 'This is the work of God, that ye believe on Him Whom He hath sent.'"[2]

"Further, these modernist ecclesiastics are warned, 'And if any man shall take away from the Words of the Book of this prophecy, God shall take away his part out of the Book of Life, and out of the Holy City, and from the things which are written in this Book.'"[3]

"However, as regards the 'synagogue of Satan,' Messiah also in the previous chapter of Revelation[4] states that He knows the blasphemy of them which say they are Jews, and are not, but are the 'synagogue of Satan.' It must be clear from these two statements, that He was foretelling the activities of the Ashkenazim, who say they are Jews, but are not of the Semitic race at all."

"Now, according to a report in the *Yorkshire Post* some years ago, Dr. Abelson, the Jewish Rabbi in Leeds, stated that the idea now permeating Jewish thought is that no personal Messiah is to be expected, but that the Jews themselves constitute the Body of Messiah which, according to the prophecies, is to rule all nations with a rod of iron."

"This idea was corroborated by a prominent international financier, who some years ago on the public platform, stated, 'We Jews are the Messiah. We have said, "Father forgive them." We are the Messiah. It might be here pointed out that he was also a Zionist."

"It would appear that this idea is the blasphemy of which Messiah was prophesying when He made the statement in question."

"But," said Brian, "surely the Book of Revelation is by St. John the Divine. I heard a sermon preached recently on a text which the preacher stated was from the Revelation of St. John the Divine."

"Not at all," Samuel replied. "Read the very first verse of Revelation which states, 'The Revelation of Jesus Christ, which God gave unto Him.' I am quite aware that the ecclesias-

---

[1] John 14: 6. [2] John 6: 29. [3] Rev. 22: 19. [4] Rev. 2: 9.

tics do call it the Revelation of St. John the Divine, but this is simply the ecclesiastical mind. Ecclesiastics formerly called themselves 'Divines,' and hence called John, 'the Divine' also, but John did not make the revelation, it was made to him, as stated in the first verse of that Book."

"However to continue: what may appear to you to be a coincidence is that Isaiah in the same chapter and verse, that is 3: 9, whilst prophesying of Jerusalem and its inhabitants, states, 'the shew of their countenance doth witness against them.' This, interpreters of prophecy have stated, refers to the hooked nose and swarthy complexion of the so-called typical Jew, and I had always agreed with this interpretation until I studied the question and obtained the ethnologists' reports to the effect that the Ashkenazim so-called Jew, who always carries these earmarks, was not of our race at all, but of the round-skulled race. Once this had been discovered, it was quite clear that Isaiah's prophecy meant that their countenance witnessed that they were NOT Jews, but are the ones whom Messiah states, 'say they are Jews, and are not, but do lie, but are the synagogue of Satan.'"

"I should like to tell you of the significance of the number '9', which occurs in both Isaiah and Revelation, when referring to these so-called Jews. Have you by any chance studied what is considered to be the modern science of numerology, but actually is a very old science which was understood by our forefathers, and which during the Babylonian Captivity degenerated into Cabalism?"

"No," Brian replied. "I know only that it has reference to numbers and their supposed meanings."

"Well," his cousin continued, "according to this ancient science, supposed to have been shown to Enoch, the seventh from Adam, and who according to many reliable sources was divinely shown the Phoenician-Hebrew alphabet, each number has a spiritual meaning. In his 'Spiritual Significance of Numbers,' Dr. Bullinger, D.D., states that the number '9', including its factors and multiples, always denotes finality of judgement. In this he is borne out by Davidson, Lawson, Nicklin, and others, in their writings on prophecy."

"At first I was very dubious as to numbers having spiritual meanings, but noting that Isaiah 3: 9, and Revelations 3: 9, were quite obviously about the same subject, and both appeared to be judgements, I began to look up in the prophetical books the judgements on Israel and Judah. I was astonished to find that in nearly all cases, the judgements were contained in verses numbered 9, or its multiples and factors, such as 18, 27, and so on."

"The great judgement on Israel appears to be given in Amos 9: 9, where Jehovah states, 'For Lo, I will command, and I will sift the House of Israel among all nations, like as corn is sifted in a sieve, yet shall not the least grain fall upon the earth.' This judgement had been in force for centuries, but finally the majority of the tribes had been gathered into Britain.

"Similarly, Hosea 1: 9 stated that Israel were to be 'Lo-ammi,' meaning 'Not My People;' whilst Isaiah 6: 9 states, 'Hear ye indeed, but understand not; and see ye indeed, but perceive not;' which would appear to be the reason for Israel's blindness as to her own identity. This judgement is rescinded, however, in Isaiah 29: 18, which states, 'In that day shall the deaf hear the words of the Book, and the eyes of the blind shall see out of obscurity and darkness.' The result of this judgement appears to be that Israel herself makes the judgement given in Isaiah 25: 9, where she states, 'Lo, this is our God; we have waited for Him and He will save us; this is Jehovah; we waited for Him, we will be glad and rejoice in His salvation.' This would appear to be the 'enquiry' called for by Israel in Ezekiel.' "[1]

"The New Testament," he continued, "also has many such judgements given in verses numbered '9' or its multiples; this being particularly apparent in St. John's writings, especially

[1] Ezek. 36: 37.

Revelation. One such final judgement in John 10: 9, is very comforting to those who have accepted Messiah as their Saviour and their Righteousness, and which states, 'I AM the Door: by Me if any man enter in, he shall be saved;' which Door He also mentions in Revelation 3: 8, whilst verse 9 gives the reward of judgement to those who enter by that Door, and also the judgement on the 'synagogue of Satan.' "

"I could go on for hours pointing out judgements given in verses numbered '9' or its multiples or factors, but we have not the necessary time, so do verify it for yourself. I should, however, like to point out that the division of Judah into 'Good Figs' and 'Evil Figs' is given us in Jeremiah, chapter 24, whilst the judgement on the 'Evil Figs' is given us in verse 9 of that chapter, which states, 'And I will deliver them to be removed into all the kingdoms of the earth for their hurt, to be a reproach and a proverb, a taunt and a curse, in all places whither I shall drive them.' You can decide for yourself whether this judgement on the Jews has been carried out, and I think that you will be glad that our ancestors had been removed from the Holy Land earlier, and were not with Zedekiah and those who remained in the land, against whom the judgement was directed."

"There is one point which rather puzzles me," Brian said. "That is that promises of great blessings were made to Israel in Deuteronomy[1] if they kept the Law of the Lord. As the Jews kept the Law, why have they been so punished and cursed, instead of having the promised blessings?"

"My dear chap," his cousin replied, "the Jews have never kept the Law of the Lord. It was for failure to keep the Law that they were deported into Babylonia. Whilst there they adopted a great many Babylonian laws, and Rabbinical writings of the ecclesiastics, with far-fetched interpretations of the Law of the Lord. These they substituted for the Law of the Lord, calling them the Talmudic law. Messiah kept the Law of the Lord, whilst the Jewish religious leaders kept the Talmudic law, with the result that they continually opposed

[1] Deut. 28: 1-15.

Him for not keeping their laws; whilst He on many occasions upbraided them for not keeping the Law of the Lord, which He had given them at Mount Sinai. He said, 'Thus have ye made the Commandment of God of none effect by your tradition;'[1] and again, 'Full well ye reject the Commandment of God, that ye may keep your tradition.'[2] His remarks, 'The poor ye have with you always,' was sarcasm, meaning that they were not keeping the Law of the Lord, as it was promised if the Law were kept that there would be no poor.[3] In the 'Sermon on the Mount,'[4] He gave His interpretation of the Law, with an added spiritual meaning.''

"The religious leaders had added greatly to the Law by their interpretations and additions, thus 'binding heavy burdens and grievous to be borne, and laying them on men's shoulders,' as Messiah said of them. They had made religion simply a matter of formal outward observances. They spent their time in senseless arguments in the name of religion. To demonstrate the ecclesiastical mind, one of their favourite subjects for argument was as to how many angels could dance together on the point of a needle, and they would spend hours arguing on the matter, and on other equally senseless matters, all in the name of religion."

"One can understand, therefore, Messiah's anger at them, and His scathing denunciations of such religious leaders for what they had done to His Divine Laws."

"The Law of the Lord consisted of natural laws in the various fields of economics, health, agriculture, criminal matters, justice, and civil government. They are apparently just as much natural laws as are the laws of gravity, fire, laws of chemistry and mathematics in their various fields, and all of which He had put into force when He created the earth, and later man. Just as one is burnt if one puts one's hand in the fire, or hurt if one falls, due to the natural laws of fire and gravity, so if Israel failed to keep the Lord's natural Laws which He gave to them, then they would suffer from working contrary to nature; whilst if they kept those natural

---

[1] Matt. 15: 6. [2] Mark 7: 9. [3] Deut. 15: 4-5. [4] Matt., Chapters 5, 6 and 7.

Laws they would have peace, health, prosperity, and blessing. Hence the Jews, who were keeping their own man-made laws and traditions, and which were contrary to the natural Laws of the Lord, could not expect the promised blessings, but instead the punishment promised if they were not kept."

"Similarly today, the Israel nations are not keeping the natural Laws of the Lord, but have followed in many instances the teachings of pseudo-scientists which are often diametrically opposed to the natural Laws."

"Protocol No. 2 of the 'Learned Elders of Zion' states that they were teaching to the 'Goyim' (Gentiles) false scientific theories to weaken them and degenerate their minds, so that we know the source of these false teachings."

"In this connection, and as I have already told you, Protocol No. 2 refers to the great success arranged for Darwinism, which is the false theory of evolution."

"But surely," Brian interposed, "Evolution has been proved, and is not simply a theory."

"In that you are absolutely wrong," Samuel replied. "It is simply a theory which has never been proved, and which has never been accepted by many of our greatest scientists. I have taken the trouble to make notes of the statements of some of our greatest scientists on the theory of evolution, so shall read them to you shortly."

Again going to his desk, he selected a notebook and returned to his chair. After finding his place, he stated:

"Here are some of the modern scientific views on this theory:

"At the annual meeting of the British Association in 1929, Professor D. M. S. Watson in his Presidential Address to the Zoological Section, said:

" 'The Theory of Evolution is a theory universally accepted, not because it can be proved to be true, but because *the only alternative*, special creation, is clearly incredible.' "

"Referring to the above statement of Dr.. Watson, Dr. Basil Atkinson stated: 'It gives the whole case for evolution away.' "

---

[1] Deut. 28: 15-66.

"In his book 'Evolution or Creation,' Sir Ambrose Fleming, M.A., D.Sc., F.R.S., states: 'There must have been at some time in the far past an act of creation of Matter, and no theory of evolution can evade this conclusion. All physicists, past and present, agree.' "

"Also the very eminent Sir James Jeans, in his book, 'Eos,' (page 35) states: 'Everything points with overwhelming force to a definite event or series of events of creation at some time or times not infinitely remote.' "

"Lord Kelvin said 'Science positively demands creation'."

"Arnold Lunne, in the *English Review*, January, 1934, says: 'We can find more support for Genesis in the Geological record than for the theories of evolutionists.' "

"He also states: 'The theory of evolution in general, and neo-Darwinism in particular, is based on a series of guesses unsupported by anything which would be regarded as evidence in a court of law: . . . evolution is nothing more than a plausible and convenient hypothesis. Its appeal is fundamentally aesthetic rather than scientific.' "

"That great scientist, himself an evolutionist, the late Yves Delage, admitted: 'If one takes one's stand upon the exclusive ground of the facts, it must be acknowledged that the formation of one species from another species has not been demonstrated at all.' "

"Of the many modern scientists who have refused the theory of evolution, a few are:

"David Brewster: 'We have absolute proof of the immutability of the species.' "

"Dr. Etheridge, famous curator of the British Museum: 'Nine-tenths of the talk of evolution is sheer nonsense founded only on observation and wholly unsupported by facts. This museum is full of the falsity of their views.' "

"Sir Charles Bell, University College, London: 'Everything declares the species to have their origin in a distinct creation, not in a gradual variation of some original type.' "

"Louis Agassiz, world-famous scientist: 'The theory is a scientific mistake, untrue in its facts, unscientific in its methods, and mischievous in its tendencies.' "

"Rudolf Virchow, famous Berlin anthropologist, was at first in favour of evolution, but later his final statement was: 'It is all nonsense, and cannot be proven.' "

"Lord Kelvin, for forty years head of the British Association of Science: 'Evolution is an absurd and impossible doctrine, a fantastic speculation.' "

"Luther Townsend, Boston University. His book against evolution is named 'The Collapse of Evolution.' "

"George F. Wright, Oberlin College, and Sir William Dawson, Canadian geologist, also wrote against evolution."

"Louis Trenchard Moore delivered ten lectures against it at Princeton University in 1924. His book is entitled 'Dogma of Evolution.' "

"Louis Pasteur, Lord Cuvier, Charles Linnaeus, Sir Roderick Murchison, Dr. Howard Kelly, Professor C. C. Everett, and Professor N. S. Shaler, as well as many others, are all on record against this theory."

"By the testimonies of evolutionists themselves they have never been able to discover any definite evidence whatever, in the records of the past or in the efforts of modern scientists, to demonstrate that evolution has really taken place. No new species have been produced, although new varieties have been produced."

"With reference to Darwin's theory that man has been evolved from the anthropoid ape, it would be interesting if evolutionists could tell us at what period this supposed evolution ceased, and why those who still remain as apes did not also evolve into men."

"The theory of Evolution," Samuel continued, "was considered for some fifty years by many scientists to be true, but during the last twenty-five years so much new knowledge of

scientific matters has come to light that at present no prominent up-to-date scientist has any faith in it. I shall read you
what W. Bell Dawson, M.A., D.Sc., F.R.S.C., states to be the
present attitude of science in his 'Opinions of Scientists on
Evolution.'" He writes:

"'It was formerly thought that our advance in knowledge
would enable us to explain everything in Nature, and how
things came to be. But this advance and further inventions have
only made things more inscrutable and mysterious. So now
investigators do not attempt to explain, but only to ascertain
how things behave under different conditions.'"

"'Our best thinkers realize that only a Being with infinite
wisdom can understand the ultimate nature of things, and how
they originated; and only so far as God has revealed them
to us, can we understand them.'"

"I must say," Brian stated, "that these statements of
scientists have greatly surprised me. I had never examined
the question, but had always taken evolution to be a proven
fact."

"This was the plan of its originators—that the public
would accept it without asking for proof. On his death-bed,
Darwin recanted, and asked his son to write a book to that
effect, which he did. It was called 'Darwin's Death-bed,' and
in it his son wrote that his father had repudiated his former
theories. Darwin told him that in his youth, he had put up
the suggestion that evolution might be the answer to many
questions. This suggestion was taken up by certain so-called
scientists, who asked him to write a book proving his theories.
He stated that, 'in the pride of my youth, I did so,' but he
now wished to state that his ideas were theories only, and that
he had never been able to get any suggestion of proof of his
theories, and repented very much on his death-bed for all the
harm he had done by putting unproved theories before the
public, as so many had accepted them as truth, whereas he
now knew them to be untrue."

Darwin's 'Origin of Species' was sold out on the day of issue. 'Darwin's Death-bed' was practically suppressed, and the public as such never heard of it, or that he had repudiated his theories. You can easily surmise who was responsible for both the 'great success' of his 'Origin of Species,' and also for the practical suppression of 'Darwin's Death-bed.' "

"It is inconceivable to my mind," said Brian, "that any persons could wilfully teach such false theories for the purpose of leading the public away from God's truth."

"It is inconceivable," Samuel replied, "to the 'seed of the woman' nations but to the 'seed of the serpent' it is the natural thing to do. They simply follow the methods of Satan, the father of lies, being his seed. It is the enmity of the 'seed of the serpent' for the 'seed of woman.'[1] The 'seed of the woman' hate to believe that anyone would do such things wilfully, so gladly accept the statement that the Protocols are a forgery; but world events have proved that the plans outlined in them are being carried out."

"It is on account of this attitude of not facing facts, but of thinking that other nations feel as we do, and prefer our ideals of peace rather than those of war, that we have twice been caught unprepared by Germany, and now again by Gog."

"Messiah said, 'For the children of this world-system (Kosmos) are wiser (shrewder in Weymouth translation) in their generation than the children of light.'[2] In other words, He is stating that the 'seed of the serpent' are more shrewd or subtle than the 'seed of the woman,' to whom He is the Light;[3] consequently He warned His disciples to be 'wise as serpents, and harmless as doves.' "[4]

"Their false teachings are particularly apparent in our financial and economic systems at present, and also in matters of health, which is the cause of most of our illnesses."

"That great scientist, Thomas Edison, after studying the results of the present day financial system, stated, 'Interest is the invention of Satan,' which is quite true. By creating

---

[1] Gen. 3: 15.   [2] Luke 16: 8.   [3] John 8: 12.   [4] Matt. 10: 16.

interest, money, a dead thing, breeds and perpetuates itself, which is contrary to natural law, and is the cause of all our financial and economic troubles. The Law of the Lord states many times that Israel must not lend on usury,[1] and usury and interest are synonymous according to the best diction- aries. Satan, being unable to create anything natural, created the idea of interest, which is unnatural, to be used by his 'synagogue of Satan' to bind Israel whenever they relin- quished the Law of the Lord. Apparently Satan cannot work within the natural laws, but can control those who do not practise natural laws."

"Unfortunately Israel have been bound by interest ever since the Bank Charter Act was passed in 1844, but the accumulated result of the compounding of interest on the national debt has only been heavily felt for the last twenty-five years; yet it will continue to grow until the governments free the people from International Finance."

"Jehovah foresaw that Israel would follow false pseudo- scientists rather than His Laws, and tells us through Isaiah, 'So on this race (Israel) I lay wonders, add wonders to won- ders, destroying its scientists' science, and baffling its scholars' researches.' "[2]

"Thank you," said Brian. "That answers my question quite clearly. There is, however, one other point I should like cleared up. You have several times stated or inferred that the Canaan- ites were the source of many of our troubles. What did you mean by that?"

"The answer is rather a long one," Samuel replied, "and would take a great deal of study and the searching of many ancient documents, finding a fact here and another there to build up the proof by corroboration. However, I shall try to explain the matter concisely, and if you are not satisfied you will have to study the matter for yourself. Who do you think was the father of Cain?"

"Why, Adam of course," Brian replied.

---

[1] Deut. 23: 19-20, etc.   [2] Isa. 29: 14 (Fenton trans.)

"That is the generally accepted conclusion, I know," replied his cousin, "but I do not think that it is correct. Adam may have been the physical father of Cain, but he certainly was not his spiritual father. In other words, Cain was not in Adam's 'image.'"

"You will not find Cain anywhere in the Book of the Generations of Adam, which is in Genesis, chapter 5. On the other hand, Cain is given a separate line of descendants in Genesis, chapter 4, which in the Hebrew is known as the 'First Toldoth of the Generations of the Heavens and the Earth,' and has nothing to do with the generations of Adam."

"The 'Book of Enoch,' to whom we have referred before as Pa-Hanok, the founder of the Phoenician-Hebrew race, and who we are told 'walked with Jehovah, and he was not, for Jehovah took him,'[1] gives the names of the twenty leaders of Satan's 'fallen angels' with the evil knowledge which each of them taught to mankind, and which made the Flood necessary, and he tells us that Gadreel was the third senior of these leaders, and that he taught mankind 'the strokes of death' and how to make war, and tells us also that 'Gadreel led astray Eve.'"[2]

"Now, in the Book of the Generations of Adam, we are told, 'And Adam lived an hundred and thirty years, and begat a son *in his own likeness, after his image,* and called his name Seth,'[3] but, as already stated, you will nowhere find Cain's name in that book of Adam's generations."

"Again, after the fall of Adam and Eve, Jehovah said to the serpent, by which the translators translated the Hebrew word 'Nachash,' meaning 'The Shining One,' 'And I will put enmity between thee and the woman, and between *thy seed and her seed;*'[4] so we see that the serpent or Satan had a 'seed' in the earth."

"Eve understood this quite clearly, as is evident from her statement on the birth of Seth, or as it is in the Hebrew, Sheth, meaning 'Appointed,' as she said, 'For Jehovah hath

[1] Gen. 5: 24. [2] Enoch 69: 6. [3] Gen. 5: 4. [4] Gen. 3: 15.

appointed me another seed instead of Abel, whom Cain slew.'[1] This shows that Abel was originally the 'seed of the woman,' who was slain by the enmity of the 'seed of the serpent.' St. John tells us, 'Not as Cain, who was of that Wicked One;'[2] whilst Messiah Himself stated, 'The tares are the children of the Wicked One.'[3] Also, as already stated, He told the so-called Jew religious leaders who continually opposed Him, that they were of their father the devil,[4] and not of His Sheep."[5]

"Let us now take Cain's own statement as to who his father was. Bristowe in 'Sargon the Magnificent,' demonstrates that Cain was Sargon, 'gon' being the Sumerian word for the Hebrew-Phoenician 'Cain,' whilst 'Sar' means 'Lord' or 'King,' as in Cae*sar*, Kai*sar*, C*z*ar, Nebuchadne*zz*ar, and even in our own 'Sir.' It is also demonstrated that Cain migrated down the Euphrates Valley about 3800 B.C. in to the lands of the Sumerians, which is evidently the Land of Nod mentioned in Genesis. There he made himself king over the aboriginal inhabitants, to whom he refers as 'blackheads' in his clay tablets of record, which have recently been discovered by archeologists. He named himself Sargon the Magnificent, and one such record shows him shaking hands with Satan in a compact by which Satan gave him temporal power in the world, provided that he served Satan and worked against Jehovah to establish Satan's world-system. It is also demonstrated how he introduced devil-worship amongst the inhabitants. This would appear to be the original 'synagogue of Satan,' which was refounded by Nimrod after the Flood."

"We must be careful not to confuse Sargon the Magnificent with the Assyrian King Sargon of some 3000 years later."

"If you visit the British Museum, you may there see some of the ancient records of Sargon the Magnificent. The translation of one such record states, 'I am Sargon the Magnificent; I am Sargon the Mighty; I am Sargon the Nazir; I am Sargon the son of Bel.' Now, Bel or Baal means Satan. We therefore have Cain's own testimony as to who his father was."

[1] Gen. 4: 25.   [2] I John 3: 12.   [3] Matt. 13: 38.   [4] John 8: 44.   [5] John 10: 26.

"It is also interesting to note that he states that he is the Nazir, as many interpreters of prophecy believe that the mark which Jehovah set in Cain's forehead[1] was the left-handed Swastika, which the Germans took as the Nazi symbol, and which represents opposition to the 'Son of Righteousness' as it turns in the opposite direction to the sun, which is His symbol. Cain's seed have used this Swastika all down the centuries."

"Now, at the Creation, Jehovah gave the dominion of the earth, or birthright to Adam. By the fall of Eve and then of Adam, Satan usurped the dominion from the Adamic race, and apparently gave it to the 'seed of the serpent' through Cain. Note how in the temptation of Messiah, Satan offered the kingdoms of the world-system (Kosmos) to Messiah if He would worship him, stating, 'For this is delivered to me; and to whomsoever I will I give it,'[2] which statement Messiah made no attempt to deny. In fact He several times refers to Satan as 'prince of this world-system' (Kosmos.)"[3]

"It was to re-establish His Own Kingdom in the earth that Jehovah called out Abraham from the world-system,[4] and through the miraculous birth of Isaac[5] and his seed through Jacob, formed the Nation of Israel, which was the Kingdom of Jehovah.[6] As Israel failed utterly to serve Jehovah and keep His natural Laws, it was necessary that He send His own Son as the 'True Seed of the Woman' to accomplish the redemption of Israel and the salvation of mankind: also as 'Son of Man' to restore man's lost dominion to him, binding the usurper Satan. This latter He will do on His return at the completion of the 'Seven Times' punishment on Israel."

"The sixth chapter of Genesis tells us a great deal about the necessity for the Flood, but unfortunately it has been badly translated, and requires some explanation. In this chapter we are told that the Sons of God married the daughters of men, and also that there were giants in the earth in those days, both of which statements require fuller explanations."

1 Gen. 4: 15.   2 Luke 4: 6.   3 John 14: 30; 16: 11.   4 Gen. 12: 1.   5 Gen. 21: 1, 18-11.
6 Exo. 19: 6.

"As regards the first statement, the word translated as 'Sons of God' is the Hebrew 'Elohim.' The late Rev. Pascoe Goard, a life-long Bible student, and one who had a great knowledge of the real meanings of the original manuscripts, and which meaning is often lost in the translations of the scribes and monks, explains in his book, 'The Names of God,' that 'Elohim' appears in the first verse of the Bible, and is apparently man's own description of God. This name is nowhere stated to have been revealed to man, as were His names of El; El Shaddai, El Elyon, Jehovah, and several other names revealed to Abraham, Isaac, Jacob, Moses, and to others. As Goard points out, Elohim is man's own idea of God, and includes His Heavenly Hosts. Further, Israel were told not to serve other elohim,[1] and in another place, not to fear the elohim of the Amorites."[2]

"Goard goes on to explain that these elohim are in two major groups; those in one group serving and worshipping the Father; whilst in the other group are those who have rebelled against the Father, and are serving Satan, with or without worship. In the case of the latter group, their aim is to make mankind serve and worship them and Satan, instead of serving and worshipping the Father."

"The 'Sons of God' referred to in the sixth chapter of Genesis were some of Satan's elohim, or 'fallen angels' who married daughters of men, by whom they had progeny who were called 'Nephilim' from the Hebrew word 'Naphal' to 'fall.' This word has been translated as 'giants,' thus losing the meaning. Actually they were giants, but the main point is that they were 'fallen ones,' who degenerated mankind by their evil deeds and rebellion against Jehovah, which they taught to mankind."

"Dr. Bullinger, D.D., in the 'Companion Bible, Part I, Appendices 23 and 25, demonstrates these matters very clearly and lucidly. He explains how these 'fallen angels' were those referred to by St. Jude[3] who 'left their first estate.' St. Jude here uses the Greek word 'oiketerion,' which elsewhere in the

---

[1] Exo. 23: 24. [2] Judges 6: 10. [3] Jude 1: 6.

New Testament is translated as 'spiritual body.' He explains
how these fallen angels left their 'spiritual bodies,' taking on
mortal bodies, and that they married the daughters of men,
and contaminated the human race, making them copy their evil
deeds and become monsters of iniquity and rebellion against
Jehovah and His Laws. Apparently the exception was in
Noah's line of descent through Enoch, who had kept their
blood-stream uncontaminated by the Nephilim blood.[1] Hence
Jehovah was forced to destroy mankind by the Flood, with
the exceptions of Noah and his sons."

"It may be said that the Nephilim were giants, being the
Anakim, Zam-Zummin, and other races of giants, to whom
Og, King of Bashan, belonged, whose bedstead was over 17
feet long.[2] Goliath of Gath, who was killed by David, was
nine feet tall.[3] They were partly supernatural, and according
to Dr. Bullinger, were the heroes of the ancient Egyptian,
Babylonian, Greek, and Roman mythologies, which accounts
for the supernatural deeds of those legendary heroes."

"Unfortunately, Noah's son Ham married Naamah, according to Bristowe's 'Sargon the Magnificent,' and Naamah was
a descendant of Cain,[4] so that the evil blood of the 'seed of
the serpent' was carried through the Flood, and she per-
petuated Cain's name in her son Canaan, who was cursed by
his grandfather Noah.[5] Ham's other sons by Naamah were
Cush, Phut, and Mitzer, the latter being the founder of Egypt.
Cush had several sons, including Nimrod the founder of Babel
after the Flood, later called Babylon, and who also is stated
to have refounded the 'synagogue of Satan.'"

"From Canaan the Canaanite nations are descended, whom
Jehovah told Israel to utterly destroy on account of their
wickedness and degeneration.[6] Unfortunately Israel failed to
do this, and the Canaanites led her astray into idolatry, and
from keeping Jehovah's Laws, thus causing her divorce from
Him, and her 'Seven Times' punishment."

"Again, we are told that when Abraham entered the Land

[1] Gen. 6: 9.   [2] Deut. 3: 11.   [3] I Sam. 17: 4.   [4] Gen. 4: 22.   [5] Gen. 9: 25.   [6] Deut. 20: 17;
Josh. 3: 10.

of Canaan, 'the Canaanite was already in the land.'[1] Dr. Bullinger demonstrates that this refers to another irruption of 'fallen angels' who had again married Canaanite women, and again formed a race of Nephilim giants who, by the time that Israel entered Canaan, had so degenerated and diseased the Canaanites that Jehovah was forced to order Israel to destroy them."

"This bringing of the 'seed of the serpent' into Israel by marriage seems to be one of Satan's main weapons against her. He tempted Esau to marry two Canaanite women,[2] but Jehovah's prescience had provided, and to keep the blood-stream of the birthright clean, He had given the birthright to Jacob.[3] Again, Satan tempted Judah to marry a Canaanite woman,[4] by whom he had three sons. Jehovah removed two of them, being childless, but allowed the third, Shelah, to remain alive, and his descendants entered the Promised Land.[5] It is probable that Adonikam and those Jewish leaders who continually opposed Messiah were of this Canaanitish line, as Messiah stated that they were of their father the devil,[6] and also that Judas Iscariot was a devil."[7]

"We can see the wisdom and love of Jehovah in thus allowing this 'seed of the serpent' in Judah, as by it Satan caused the sacrifice of Messiah, thus 'Making an end of sins,'[8] and thereby Satan brought about his own downfall. Messiah thus redeemed His Israel, saved mankind, and on His return will bind Satan, as Israel will then 'know Him from the least of them unto the greatest of them,' and will at last recognize the difference between Jehovah's truth and Satan's lies, and will follow her God, for He will abundantly pardon."[9]

"Haberman in 'Tracing Our Ancestors,' demonstrates that the Latin races of Europe are the descendants of the Canaanite nations; whilst Nimrod's descendants, the Babylonians, were in the German Reich. The Prussians, however, according to a Prussian secular professor, Professor Swaner, are the descendants of the Assyrians, or Assur as it is in the Hebrew,

---

[1] Gen. 12: 6. [2] Gen. 26: 34. [3] Gen. 25: 23. [4] Gen. 38: 1. [5] I Chron. 4: 21. [6] John 8: 44. [7] John 6: 70. [8] Dan. 9: 24. [9] Isa. 55: 7.

who were originally conquered by Nimrod, but who later
obtained their freedom, and conquered and deported Ten-
Tribed Israel.[1] Soon afterwards Assyria was again conquered
by Babylon, and has apparently since been associated with her."

"A peculiar thing is that Assur or Assyria was a descendant of Shem, and therefore Semitic; whilst Nimrod and his
followers were Hamitic, and through Ham's wife, Naamah,
show the differently-shaped head, which caused our men to
call them 'square-heads' and Huns, in which they were correct."

"The Prussians, on the other hand, are long-skulled, being
Semitic like Israel, and they were the leaders of Germany until
Hitler and his Nazis obtained control. Even during Hitler's
régime they were in most cases the Army leaders. It is interesting to note that in his writings, Professor Swaner, after
stating that the Prussians are the descendants of the Assyrians, concludes, 'Hence our hereditary hatred of the English,
who are the descendants of Israel.' "

"Jehovah tells us in Ezekiel[2] that He will bring Gog against
His land, stating that Gog is the one whom all the prophets
prophesied would be brought against Israel,[3] so that it would
appear that the prophecies of Joel, Zechariah, Ezekiel, and the
other prophets regarding the taking of Jerusalem by the
Northern Army and the destruction of that army, all refer
to Gog's attack. Further, the Revised, Fenton, and other
translations all state that Cush and Phut will be with Gog,
and not Ethiopia and Libya, as stated in the Authorized
Version."

"Now, as already stated, Cush was the father of Nimrod,
founder of Babylon, which finally was represented by the
German Reich, so that we can see that the prophets stated
that the remnant of Germany would be with Gog."

"According to prophecy, this Northern Army is to be
destroyed by Jehovah, but Ezekiel tells us that Jehovah states
that He 'will yet be enquired of by the House of Israel to do
it for them.'[4] Further, it is as a result of that supernatural

---

[1] II Kings 17: 6.   [2] Ezek. 38 and 39.   [3] Ezek. 38: 17 (Fenton trans.)   [4] Ezek. 36: 37.

destruction that 'so the House of Israel shall know that I AM JEHOVAH their God from that day and forward:'[1] 'I AM' being the name of Jehovah.[2] This 'enquiry' is probably the one where Israel states, 'Our hands NO victory won: the world's men did NOT fall.' "[3]

"We can therefore see that Gog's attack is the signal that the curtain has gone up for the final scene in the 'Seven Times' punishment on Israel, and that it means that the 'Times of the Gentiles' is to end and that, as told us in Zechariah's fourteenth chapter, Messiah is to return to set up His Kingdom of God in Israel, and which is to spread until He is again King of the earth."[4]

"It is therefore quite probable that if your Chief leaves you in Palestine for long, that you will see the destruction of Gog's army, and shortly afterwards Messiah's return and the setting up of His Kingdom."

Brian, who had been looking at his watch for some minutes, said, "You have certainly given me a most interesting evening, Samuel. I had no idea that it was so late. It is after midnight, and I fear that I have been keeping you from your rest. I must rush, as I have an early start before me in the morning."

Samuel prevailed on his cousin to have a final nightcap, whilst he wrote a letter of introduction for Brian to Amos Ben Jacob, his intimate friend in Jerusalem; after receiving which Brian left with the hearty good wishes of his cousin ringing in his ears.

---

[1] Ezek. 39: 22. [2] Exo. 3: 14. [3] Isa. 26: *18* (Fenton trans.) [4] Zech. 14: *9*.

CHAPTER IV.

"TRAVELOGUE."

Next morning Brian was at the aerodrome bright and early, and had a short wait before his plane took off.

In the adjoining seat was an army officer with whom he got into conversation. The officer was going to Palestine to take up a staff appointment, and was full of Gog's attack.

It had become public knowledge that the Zionists were in some way responsible for Gog's attack, and the officer was very bitter in his remarks against the Jews.

After listening for some minutes, Brian cut him short, saying, "Look here! I myself am of Jewish Sephardim blood, but neither I nor any of my blood so far as I know have had anything to do with Gog's attack. You do not appear to realize that there are two races of so-called Jews, the Sephardim, or true Semitic Jew of Israel blood, and the Ashkenazim from Eastern Europe who are not Semitic, nor are they Jews except by religion. In fact the ethnologists will tell you that the Sephardim are long-skulled and of the Mediterranean race, whilst the Ashkenazim are round-skulled and of the Alpine race. It is entirely the Zionist Party who claim the Holy Land, and who are connected with Gog's attack, and the Zionists are controlled by the Ashkenazim and others who are not of true Semitic blood. The Sephardim do not claim the Holy Land, nor do they belong to the Zionist Party, except perhaps in some individual cases."

The officer replied, "I must certainly apologize for my remarks, and for my ignorance of the details of the Jewish question. If you don't mind my saying so, I should never have taken you for a Jew. Your eyes are blue; your hair auburn; and your nose quite small and straight. I hope that you will forgive me."

Brian gladly accepted his apology, and added, "As regards your remarks about my eyes being blue, my hair reddish, and my nose straight, you will find when you arrive in Palestine that the Jews whose ancestors have never left the Holy Land have in the majority of cases blue eyes, light hair, and straight well-cut noses. On the other hand, you will find that the newly-arrived Zionists have in most cases black hair, dark eyes, and the hooked nose which unfortunately in the opinion of the public is characteristic of the Jew. Actually it is just the opposite, being the sign that the owner is Ashkenazim, and therefore not a Jew at all, but for purposes of his own is masquerading as one to attain world control through the falsely-named Zionism."

The officer appeared to be most interested and asked for further information on the subject. Brian thereupon gave him a short resumé of what his cousin had told him of the Ash-kenazim and the Zionist Party, with its "secret advisers" to our governments; its effort to discredit the Bible by its self-conceived theories of evolution, Higher Criticism, and Modern-ism, which under the name of 'scholarship' had been swallowed by many religious leaders.[1] Finally he came to the subject of international finance, as controlled by international Jewry, but here the officer, who was named Nevin, interrupted, saying, "Yes. I know something about their financial workings. A few days ago I received from a friend in Canada, a copy of the official Hansard of the 'Standing Committee on Banking and Commerce, 1939,' which shows very clearly the hold that international finance has over the people of Canada; and I understand that they have foisted similar systems on all the countries which they control."

Nevin took a book from his suitcase, and continued, "If you don't mind, I should like to read you a few extracts from the official Hansard in question, as the fact that it is an official government document, and that the answers are by the Gover-nor of the Bank of Canada, a Mr. Graham F. Towers, and by the Deputy Minister of Finance, a Dr. W. C. Clark, make it truly authentic."

---

[1] Protocol of Zion, No. 2.

"Here are a few extracts from the Hansard which may interest you:"

"On page 42, Dr. Clark states: 'Bank deposits constitute by far the largest portion of our money.'"

"On pages 43 and 285, both Clark and Towers state: 'It is the bank deposit (credit at the bank) itself which constitutes money.'"

"On page 286 it is stated: 'It is not necessary that there be in existence a dollar of physical money (coins and notes) for every dollar of deposits. Quite the contrary. Actually the total of bank deposits runs four to five times the amount of physical money in existence.'"

"On page 286, Towers further states: 'It is not correct to say that a bank deposit is "Just as good as money," or that it is a "substitute for money." A bank deposit or "credit at the bank" actually is money—it is the major kind of money— it is the kind of money with which 95 per cent of business is done.'"

Nevin added, "Notice that it makes no difference whether the deposit or 'credit at the bank' has been created by handing in bank notes, etc., or by simply negotiating a loan—in either case it is a deposit—a credit—money."

"Who creates money?" he continued. "Page 287 of Hansard tells us officially, and states: 'But there is no question about it that banks *create* that medium of exchange?'"

"Answer by Towers: 'That is right. That is what they are for.'"

"Question: 'And they issue that form of medium of exchange *when they purchase securities* or *make loans?*'"

"Answer: 'That is the banking business, just in the same way that a steel plant makes steel.' 'Steal' is a most applicable word," Nevin added.

"Both Clark and Towers state on pages 76 and 238, that the 'manufacturing process' consists of making a pen and ink or typewriter entry in a book or on a card."

"Towers further states on pages 113 and 238: 'Each and every time a bank makes a loan (or purchases securities) new bank credit is created—new deposits—brand new money.'"

"As confirmed by Mr. Towers, we are told on page 123: 'The bulk of the deposits arise out of the action of the banks themselves, for, by granting loans, allowing money to be drawn on an overdraft, or purchasing securities, a bank creates a credit on its books, which is the equivalent of a deposit.' And," Nevin added, "a 'deposit' is 'money' as defined above."

"We can therefore see," Nevin said, "that most of our 'money' has no physical existence at all—except as 'figures in a book,' but we pay interest on the securities so purchased by the bank, and on the loans they make both to the government and to private individuals. It certainly is a terrible 'racket,' and I cannot see why the governments do not issue their own 'money,' and ignore the banks' money."

"The 'secret advisers' to the governments on financial matters," Brian interjected, "see to it that the governments do not do so,"

"Yes," Nevin said. "In Protocol of Zion No. 8 it is stated, 'Around us again will be a whole constellation of bankers, industrialists, capitalists, and—the main thing—millionaires, because in substance everything will be settled by the question of figures.' It took them many years to accomplish it, but from the present-day financial system, it is quite clear that they have made 'money' simply a matter of 'figures in a book.'"

"It is a terrible situation," he continued, "when as Edison, the great American inventor, said, 'People who will not turn a shovel full of dirt, nor contribute a pound of material, will collect more money from the United States than will the people who supply all the material and do all the work. That is the terrible thing about interest. Under the present system of doing business, we simply add from 120 per cent to 150 per cent to the stated cost. Interest is the invention of Satan.'"

"He is right there," Brian replied. "It is the invention of
the 'synagogue of Satan,' and contrary to the Law of the
Lord."[1]

"Here are a few more extracts from Hansard which might
interest you," Nevin continued. "On pages 461 and 794
Towers states: 'Broadly speaking, all new "money" comes out
of a bank in the form of loans.' On page 459, he also tells us
that under the present system ALL 'MONEY' IS DEBT.
This means debt on the part of the public to the banks and,
as it is in the form of loans, that debt is at interest."

"Again, we are told on page 7 by Dr. Clark, and on page
102 by Mr. Towers that for each dollar of gold which a bank
holds they may issue $4.00 in paper banknotes, whilst for each
of these dollars in paper banknotes, they may issue $19.00 in
credit, on all of which credit they may charge interest. That
is for $1.00 in gold they may issue $80.00 in credit at interest."

"This means that for each 1¼c of gold which they hold,
the bank may issue $1.00 in credit, or to purchase securities
on which, at the present rates of interest, if invested in government securities the government, which is the public, would
pay some 2¾ per cent, or more than twice the value of the
gold with which the banks back their $1.00 in credit. If loaned
to a private individual, the bank would charge some 5 per cent
or 6 per cent, or about four times the amount of their gold
backing behind the loan. A nice game, isn't it?"

"Now, according to the present government ruling, only
the government or a chartered bank may possess gold bullion.
The banks pay somewhere around $38.00 per ounce of gold,
but with $38.00 worth of gold they may issue 80 x $38.00, or
slightly over $3000 in credit AT INTEREST. Do you wonder
that business cannot prosper, when the government must so
raise taxation to meet interest created by such methods?"

"Had I not read these facts in an official government Hansard, I would not have believed that any government would
allow the financial interests to operate in such a way."

[1] Deut. 23: 19-20.

"It is by the piling up and compounding of such interest that our Democratic countries have such huge national debts, with the result that the governments burden us with sales taxes, 'nuisance taxes,' and taxes on almost everything in order to pay the interest to international finance; which taxes keep the people poor, allow no chance for the expansion of industry, and thus cause unemployment. Heavy taxes, caused by paying interest on the national debts, are the fundamental cause of unemployment and low wages. Labour considers that low wages are the fault of the employer in industry, but this is entirely wrong. The fault is from heavy taxes, which do not allow the employer to pay good wages, and the heavy taxes are necessary and will be necessary to pay interest, until the governments issue their own money, cancel the government guarantees on the banks' paper currency, and cancel the privilege of the banks to issue credit on 'figures in a book.' "

"Prior to 1844, when the Bank Charter Act was put through, the national debt was comparatively small," Nevin continued, "and now it has reached astronomical proportions but, as shown by the Hansard, it is in figures only and means nothing, provided that the government would issue its own currency, and completely ignore international finance."

Taking his pocketbook from his pocket, he selected a paper, and said, "I should like to read you a short extract from an editorial in the *London Times*, written years ago when Abraham Lincoln first issued government paper money. It states: 'If this mischievous financial policy, which had its origin in the North American Republic, should become endurated down to a fixture, then that government will furnish its own money WITHOUT COST. It will pay off its debts and be WITHOUT DEBTS. It will have all the money necessary to carry on its commerce. It will become prosperous beyond precedent in the history of the world. The brains and wealth of all countries will go to North America. That government must be destroyed, or it will destroy every monarchy in the world.' "

"Shortly after the publication of this editorial, the National Bank Act was 'railroaded' through the United States Congress in 1863, and the Americans have since been controlled by International Finance. Of course everyone realizes that the issuance of currency by the government would in no way affect any monarchy, except that of International Finance, which it would naturally destroy. The editorial I have quoted has always been attributed to the Rothschild interests."

"Yes," Brian replied, "my cousin who is prominent in Sephardim Jewish affairs, but who has nothing to do with International Finance, has a good knowledge of their system. He considers that it is the 'synagogue of Satan' who are the 'hidden heads' of the financial system."

"From the 'Protocols of the Learned Elders of Zion,' which I read recently," Nevin continued, "it is the Zionist Party who control the financial system, or at least so they claim in the Protocols. They have stated that the Protocols are a forgery, and have tried to have their issue prohibited; but the final result was that the Geneva Supreme Court dismissed their case and charged them 30,000 francs in costs. By the way, have you read the Protocols?"

"No," replied Brian, "but peculiarly enough my cousin was reading extracts from them to me last night. He said that the Zionists called themselves the 'Symbolic Snake' and the 300 'hidden heads' of the organization, the 'Head of the Snake.' As he pointed out, Satan is known in the Bible as the 'serpent,' or snake. My cousin accordingly considered that the 'Head of the Snake' was simply another name for what in the Bible is referred to as the 'synagogue of Satan.'"

"That appears to be most logical," Nevin replied. "I had not given the matter much thought before, but I do remember that the 300 leaders are referred to as the 'Head of the Snake.' Do you know anything about the 'synagogue of Satan,' as you have mentioned it several times?"

"No," Brian replied, "except that one of my former commanding officers told me that he had spent some twenty years in trying to trace their activities, probably for 'Intelligence,' although he never admitted that he was a member of that service. He said that they controlled the international financial system, and were responsible for all of our financial and economic troubles. Also my cousin, with whom I dined last night, said that so far as he was able to ascertain, the organization was controlled by the Ashkenazim section of the Zionist Party."

"That seems to be about all that any outsider knows about them," Nevin said, "but if your cousin is correct, and his ideas on the subject seem to be most logical; then the 'Head of the Snake' and the 'synagogue of Satan' are identical; in which case the Protocols give us a very full outline of their activities. Further, the Protocols have clearly defined beforehand what world events were to be from 1905, when they were brought to light, until the present day, and the events which they then defined have now become world history. This would indicate that their plans have been successfully carried out to date, and that therefore it must have been the actual plans of the Zionists which were outlined in the Protocols."

"I must read the Protocols," said Brian. "Have you, by any chance a copy with you?"

"Unfortunately, I have not," Nevin replied, "but I know the address of the publishers of the Marsden edition. Marsden was the British newspaper correspondent who smuggled the copy which he obtained out of Russia in 1905 and which original copy is now, I believe, in the British Museum. The Britons Publishing Society, 40 Great Ormond St., London, W.C. 1, are the publishers."

Brian thanked him, making a note of the address, and they continued to chat on various subjects. Both were old travellers who had done much travel by air, so spent little time in trying to watch the scenery, particularly as their plane travelled at a high altitude, but instead discussed the world situation, descending from their plane to take exercise at the various intermediate airports en route.

Brian related some of the facts which his cousin had told him the previous evening regarding the Anglo-Saxon-Celtic nations being the descendants of Israel and Judah. He soon found that Nevin had already studied the British-Israel theory and firmly believed in it. However, he had never before heard the facts regarding the main part of Judah having migrated into Britain, Northern Ireland, and Scotland.

"This," he said, "makes the Union Jack a more interesting flag than ever. We British-Israelites had seen that the Union Jack denoted the Union of Jacobus, or Jacob, the father of the Tribes of Israel, but we thought that it signified the union of Ten-Tribed Israel only. Now it is apparent that the Cross of St. Andrew for Scotland represents Judah, whilst the Cross of St. Patrick for Ireland must represent the House of David, a part of Judah, as David was given a separate House.[1] Also the Harp of David in the Royal Standard represents Northern Ireland, and it stands for the House of David."

"In that case it means that the prophecy of Ezekiel, to the effect that Jehovah will reunite all Israel under one king,[2] has been fulfilled, and that all the tribes except Manasseh in the United States, are under one King of the House of David. I suppose that Manasseh will not join us until Our Lord returns as King, and takes the Throne of His father David, when all tribes will be under Him, as the 'Whole House of Israel.' "

"It is a most peculiar thing that the British-Israel theory is scoffed at by most people, due principally to the teachings of the organized church, who do not wish to have their self-assumed name of Israel taken from them. However, I suppose that that is why Our Lord prophesied that the Gospel of the Kingdom would be preached *as a witness* just before His return,[3] which implies that it would be refused nationally."

"Nevertheless, Our Lord also prophesied that He would

---

[1] II Sam. 7: 16.   [2] Ezek. 37: 19-22.   [3] Matt. 24: 14.

bring all nations against Jerusalem,[1] and that He would judge them there,[2] and as all nations of any importance are with Gog and against Israel, the awakening of Israel as to her identity as prophesied by Ezekiel,[3] should take place at Armageddon very shortly."

The journey passed very quickly, as both were interested in the subjects under discussion. Before they realized where they were, their plane was making its final landing at the airport outside of Jerusalem, having seen nothing of any hostile aircraft throughout the flight.

---

[1] Zech. 14: 2.   [2] Joel 3: 12.   [3] Ezek. 39: 22.

CHAPTER V.

Gog Takes Jerusalem.

Brian found a car awaiting him at the airport, which soon took him to Jerusalem and deposited him at G.H.Q.

There he reported to the officer in charge of Intelligence, Col. Smythe, who was expecting him. After enquiring as to whether he had had an eventful trip, Col. Smythe asked for his credentials, which of course were in order.

Brian then produced his letter of introduction to the G.O.C., so was taken to his office at once.

After shaking hands, the G.O.C. told him to be seated whilst he read the letter of introduction. When he had digested its contents, he turned to Brian, saying, "Before I came to the Holy Land, I should never have taken you to be of Jewish extraction. Since then, however, I have realized that the true Jew is of a very different type from the one which in Europe we consider to be the typical Jew, and that the latter type is not Semitic at all."

"It is to enquire into the activities of the latter type," he continued, "that I requested your chief to send me someone whom I could trust, and at the same time, who would be trusted by the true Jews of Jerusalem and of the Land, and who would consequently be able to work hand in glove with them. Do you think that you will be able to insinuate yourself into their confidence?"

"I think so, sir," Brian replied. "My cousin gave me a strong letter of introduction to Amos Ben Jacob, who was a very intimate friend of his when he was carrying out some researches in Jerusalem a few years ago. I believe that Amos Ben Jacob is one of the leaders of the Semitic Jews, as opposed to the Zionists in Jerusalem."

"Good," said the G.O.C., "Amos Ben Jacob is very well thought of by both the Jews and ourselves, and I feel sure that he is absolutely trustworthy, so that if you are in his confidence and have his help, we may gain some very valuable information from his associates and their subordinates as to the secret activities of the Zionists."

The G.O.C. gave Brian details of some of these secret activities which had already been unearthed, and which gave him a basis on which to commence his investigations; after receiving which Brian returned to Smythe's office. The latter arranged with him a secret system of intercommunication which would obviate the necessity of having him appear at G.H.Q. to report any information which he might acquire.

When these arrangements had been completed, he took his hand baggage with him in an army car to the bus depot, where he remained until the arrival of a bus. He then joined the stream of passengers, secured a taxi, and drove to the address of Amos Ben Jacob.

On his arrival at Amos Ben Jacob's, he found that he was expected, as Samuel had sent a cable. Amos greeted him effusively, stating how pleased he was to meet a cousin of Samuel, and insisted that his home must be Brian's whilst the latter was in Jerusalem. As this suited his plans, Brian accepted with pleasure, and soon Amos and he were chatting like old friends.

Amos gave him a resumé of the Zionists' activities, and explained that there was great animosity between the real Semitic Jews and the greater part of the Zionists whom, he stated, were usurpers of Gentile blood. He admitted that some of the Zionists were real Jews, but added that very few of their leaders had a drop of Semitic blood in them.

Brian made mental notes of the names of such of the Zionists as were the principal trouble-makers, and also of what their activities had been.

When Amos had finished the recital of his troubles with the Zionists, he immediately launched into his views on the situation in the Holy Land, pointing out how the prophecies were being fulfilled, particularly those of Ezekiel, Joel, and Zechariah.

"Gog will be destroyed," he stated. "At Megiddo will be the 'Battle of Gog's Defeat.' Israel will be at the point of defeat. Then will the Arm of Our God be revealed. Jehovah of Hosts will rain fire and brimstone on His enemies. 'I shall leave but a sixth part of thee,' He has told Gog through Ezekiel.[1] Yes, but first must the 'abomination of desolation' stand in the Holy Place.[2] Does this mean that Gog must first take Jerusalem?"

Brian replied that he could not say, as he did not understand the prophecies. He tried to change the subject, but Amos had immersed himself in his thoughts and did not appear interested in further talk.

Brian spent several days in trying to unravel the activities of the Zionists, with which he had some success. He was able to send some rather valuable information to Smythe, which enabled 'Intelligence' to nip some of their activities in the bud, and to apprehend the perpetrators.

Shortly afterwards Smythe sent word that the G.O.C. wished to see Brian. The latter reported promptly, and the G.O.C., who was up to his eyes in work and had his desk covered with reports, started in without preamble, saying, "The enemy has advanced so rapidly and is in such strength that he has easily pushed aside our advanced troops. Consequently I fear that it is too late to use you much longer in Jerusalem for the purpose which I had intended."

"I have already decided to evacuate Jerusalem so far as our own forces are concerned, and shall leave the local defence to the Semitic Jews, who insist on defending their Holy Places, and so refuse to withdraw with us. I have issued orders for the taking up of a defensive position along the southwesterly side of the Valley of Jezreel and the Plains of Megiddo, with our left flank near Haifa."

"Gog is in such strength that I do not believe that he will

---

[1] Ezek. 39: 2.   [2] Dan. 9: 27; 12: 11; Matt. 24: 15.

do more than detach a portion of his forces to attack us, but will continue his advance on Jerusalem with his main body, as our agents state that the plans of the Zionists are to have their 'Secret Leader' crowned in Zion before the Feast of Trumpets."

"It is possible that they may completely ignore our force, which is so relatively small, in which case I shall attack their communications."

"Should they attack us in great strength, however, I shall be forced to fight a withdrawal action to cover Haifa, and hope for a second miracle as at Dunkirk to get my troops embarked under cover of the Navy. Gog's preponderance in aircraft will be a great hindrance to us in any case."

"However, now that you have established yourself in the confidence of the Semitic Jews and are obtaining their assistance, I wish you to remain in Jerusalem for as long as possible, sending me any important information by the channels which Smythe tells me he has arranged with you."

Brian saw that he was dismissed, so returned to Smythe's office, but found that headquarters was being moved immediately to the rear of the defensive position near Haifa, and that Smythe was too busy to give him any detailed information. They therefore arranged that Brian would keep in touch with Amos Ben Jacob for as long as possible, and that any communications to him would be sent through that channel.

Having completed his arrangements, Brian returned to Amos Ben Jacob's house, where Amos was expecting him.

The news that the Army was being moved into a defensive position near the Plains of Megiddo had become public, and although it appeared that Jerusalem was being left to its fate, Amos was jubilant.

"What did I tell you?" he said. "Did I not say that the 'Battle of Gog's Defeat'[1] would be at Megiddo? I wonder whether the commander knows the prophecies, or is he unconsciously led there to fight?"

Brian said that it was a sign of the weakness of our forces

---
[1] Ezek. 39 : 11 (Fenton trans.)

as compared with Gog's great strength, and that we could do little else but withdraw to where there was a possibility of a successful evacuation being carried out.

"It does not matter," Amos continued. "It is Jehovah of Hosts, the God of our fathers, Who will destroy Gog. Soon will the Arm of Jehovah be revealed in destroying these Ashkenazim who usurp the land which He gave to His People, and who by falsehood take the land from His People."

Brian said that he hoped that Amos was right and that he wished that he had Amos' confidence, as he himself had deep misgivings over the whole situation.

As he had a report to write and a code to commit to memory before he could destroy it, Brian said good-night to his host and retired to his room.

Next morning news was received that Gog's advanced forces had reached Aiath, Migron, and Michmash, and were burning and destroying everything in their path.[1]

The leaders of the Semitic Jews in Jerusalem had ordered a fast, and the trumpet was blown, calling for an assembly of every soul in Jewry. The priests mourned loudly and were calling on Jehovah to spare His People;[2] whilst the area around the "Wailing Wall" was crowded with Jews, all weeping and wailing.

Late in the morning news was received that the enemy had reached Anatoth,[3] which they had burned, slaughtering such of the inhabitants as had remained there.

Amos had returned to his house, and ordered his wife and family to flee, advising Brian to accompany them. He said, "Jerusalem must be taken. Zechariah was told by Jehovah that Jerusalem was to become a 'Cup of Trembling,' and that He would cut to pieces all who burden themselves with it.[4] It is as a result of Gog taking Jerusalem, and the abominations he practises in Jerusalem that Jehovah destroys him. I have told this to the other leaders, but they will not believe me,

---

[1] Isa. 10: 28; Joel 2: 3.   [2] Joel 2: 15-16.   [3] Isa. 10: 30.   [4] Zech. 12: 2-3.

and will therefore be killed or captured. We must leave them to their fate."

Brian decided to accompany Amos in his flight from Jerusalem. He considered that if he took his field glasses with him, and secured a commanding position on the Mount of Olives that he would be able to observe Gog's advance, and his dispositions on reaching Jerusalem, which might be of interest to "Intelligence."

He communicated his idea to Amos, and asked to be given a haversack of food sufficient to last him for a couple of days.

Amos said, "Do not go to the Mount of Olives. Zechariah states that Jehovah is to rest His feet on the Mount of Olives, and to cleave it from east to west by a great valley.[1] Go rather to the high ground south of the Valley of Hinnom where you will be safer from Gog's troops, and whence you can see what transpires."

Although Brian had little fear of the Mount of Olives cleaving in two, he did think it good advice to keep on the side of Jerusalem that was farthest from the enemy and, as Amos told him of a good vantage point on commanding ground to the south of the Valley of Hinnom whence he could overlook Jerusalem, he took his advice.

Brian parted company with Amos and his family when they had arrived some distance outside the city, after arranging where they could again get into touch with each other, and started to climb to the vantage point which Amos had pointed out to him before they parted.

Before he had reached his position, he heard a burst of firing from the direction of the city, followed by desultory firing for a time. He quickened his pace up the hill to reach the position from which he could see Jerusalem.

On reaching his vantage point, he scanned with his glasses the country to the north of Jerusalem, but could see no signs of the enemy, although he could see dense masses of smoke arising from many burning villages in the distance.

[1] Zech. 14: 4.

He then turned his glasses on Jerusalem, where he saw bodies of marching men in the streets. Others appeared to be running away from them, and many were hurrying from the city, some carrying bundles, whilst a considerable number of women and children seemed to be among them.

This was puzzling to Brian, as there were no signs of Gog's mobile troops in sight of the city, so that the marching men could not be from his forces.

Shortly afterwards he saw dust moving a few miles north of Jerusalem, and soon was able to make out several patrols of tanks or other armoured fighting vehicles, which were approaching rapidly. They halted to the north of a rise in the ground some distance from the city, and apparently made a reconnaissance, during which other and larger formations of armour came into sight, and halted under cover a few hundred yards behind their advanced patrols.

Whilst he was watching these proceedings through his glasses, he noticed a large body of men marching out of the city towards the enemy's patrols, and carrying a banner on which appeared to be the Zionist emblem. Then, for the first time, he noticed that the British flag over Jerusalem had been replaced by the Zionist flag.

He watched until the marching men had arrived within a few hundred yards of the hostile patrols, where they halted whilst three of their number approached the patrols and appeared to confer with the enemy.

After a few minutes, the patrols advanced towards the halted men, whilst the larger formations of armoured fighting vehicles moved up and occupied the ridge which had been evacuated by the patrols.

When the patrols reached the halted men, the latter turned about and moved back to the city, followed by the patrols, who also entered the city.

In the meantime other formations of armour had appeared in the distance, and were rapidly approaching. Apparently the patrols who had entered the city had wirelessed back the "all clear," as the various formations in rear moved directly into the city, where Brian could see the armoured vehicles being parked in the various squares.

By dusk a large force had entered the city, whilst many more armoured formations were in parks outside the suburbs.

Just before darkness fell, the sound of heavy gunfire or bomb explosions was heard in the distance, coming from the direction of Megiddo.

As he could observe nothing further, Brian decided to give up his vigil until daylight, so set out for a house hidden in the nearby hills, and owned by a Semitic Jew, to whom Amos had given him a note of introduction, as a brother Jew who was anti-Zionist.

Brian had a luminous compass on his wrist, and had taken a bearing on the house before darkness fell, so had little trouble in keeping his direction, and after a great deal of stumbling, reached his destination.

The house appeared to be in darkness and untenanted, but Brian found a window by feeling along the wall, and was able to discern a small gleam of light behind heavy screens. He felt his way to the door, on which he was forced to knock several times before he received any answer.

Finally after some fumbling, the door was opened a few inches, and from the darkness a voice asked what he wanted.

Brian stated that he was a friend of Amos and that he had a note from him, which he had already taken from his pocket, and handed it to the owner of the voice. The latter closed the door, and Brian could hear him walking away.

After a wait of a minute or two, the door was again opened, but widely this time, and he was told to enter. The owner of the voice took his arm and led him across a room, where he felt for and found a door, which he opened and ushered him

into a lighted room where two men were sitting, who rose as
he entered.

One of them came forward and introduced himself as Haggai
Ben Aaron, to whom Amos had written the note. He also
introduced the other man as Zalthiel, an inhabitant of Jerusalem who had fled from the city that morning; and who was
also a close friend of Amos.

He then told the man wno had ushered Brian into the house
to bring refreshments, so Brian concluded that the latter
must be a servant.

After the refreshments had been brought and the man had
retired from the room, Brian asked for the latest news from
Jerusalem.

Haggai told him that when the enemy had arrived within
a few miles of the city, the Zionist organizations suddenly
opened fire on those of the Jews who did not belong to their
party, and whom the Zionists outnumbered two to one. They
had killed many of the Sephardim and other Jews who opposed
them, and had driven the remainder from the city. After this,
they had either joined Gog's forces or surrendered the city
to them, but he was not sure which of these courses they had
adopted. However, the result appeared to be the same in either
case, as Jerusalem was now under Gog's complete dominance.

They discussed the situation for awhile, and then Haggai
showed Brian to his room. Brian thanked him, adding that
as he intended to be back at his vantage point by daylight, he
must rise early.

As he was retiring, he noticed that the sound of heavy
firing to the north still continued.

During the night he was awakened by the sound of knocking at the outer door, and shortly afterwards he heard
the sound of hushed voices. Being tired, he soon fell asleep
again, and the next thing he heard was someone knocking at his
own door. He said, "Come in," and the man who had let him
into the house the night before came in carrying a lamp,

which he placed on the table. He told Brian that it was an hour before dawn, and that breakfast would be ready in a few minutes, and after lighting Brian's candle, left the room.

Brian rose, and as he was dressing noticed that the sound of heavy firing still kept up in the distance.

Brian soon dressed and went downstairs, where he found that a third man had joined Haggai and Zalthiel. The new arrival was introduced to him by Haggai as Zadok, a friend who lived in Jerusalem, and who had escaped from the city during the night.

Zadok told him that after Gog's forces had taken over the city, they had posted large proclamations in prominent places, which were printed in three languages, Hebrew, Magogian, and Arabian, to the effect that at noon the following day Gog would be crowned as "Sovereign Lord of all the World"; the ceremony to take place in front of the Mosque of Omar on Mount Moriah.

Haggai interjected, "This will be the 'abomination of desolation' standing in the Holy Place, as prophesied by Daniel the prophet.[1] You did well to flee, Zadok." To these views both Zalthiel and Zadok agreed strongly.

Zadok then stated that a high platform was being built in front of the Mosque of Omar (known as the "Dome of the Rock"), on which an exalted throne was being constructed for Gog.

Brian ate a hearty breakfast and, after thanking his host for his hospitality and also for an invitation to return later, left for his observation point.

---

[1] Dan. 9: 27; 12: 11; Matt. 24: 15.

CHAPTER VI.

"Jerusalem—A Cup of Trembling." (Zech. 12: 2.)

As dawn was breaking, Brian had no difficulty in reaching his position, and was soon studying the scene through his glasses.

Soon the sun rose and its rays revealed a huge stage or platform in front of the "Dome of the Rock," whilst on the stage itself a high throne had been constructed. The throne glittered in the light of the sun, and Brian could see workmen still at work on it, covering it with a shining yellow material, which he took to be gold.

Jerusalem appeared to be crowded with men in the uniform of the Magogian Army, whilst the area about the city was filled with parked tanks and other armoured fighting vehicles, as well as transport. All the squares in the city, except those near the temple area, were also crowded with armoured vehicles, whilst to the north there were huge concentrations of armour and transport as far as the eye could see. Gog had arrived in strength.

It soon became very hot in the sun, so Brian took shelter under some nearby trees, where he listened to the heavy firing in the distance, returning from time to time to watch the scene below.

Long before noon the large temple area began to fill, and shortly afterwards men in uniform commenced to take their places on the platform.

Brian was surprised to find that the Zionist flags were still flying over Jerusalem, and that they had not been replaced by Magogian flags. He was still more surprised to notice that a large Zionist banner had been set up in the centre of the platform in front of the throne, and for the first time realized that Gog[1] who was to be crowned was not the well-known dictator of Magog, but was actually the secret and hidden leader

[1] Ezek. 38: 2.

of the "Head of the Snake," mentioned in the "Protocols of Zion," who had secretly been controlling the dictator.

By half an hour before noon the temple area was packed with a solid mass of humanity, of which the majority were in the Magogian uniform, whilst the stage itself was also crowded, but here the proportion of those in uniform was small.

At a few minutes before noon music was heard and a procession filed on to the stage, headed by a figure dressed in a scarlet robe which glittered and threw off light in the bright rays of the sun. To the right rear of this figure was a lesser figure, also dressed in gleaming robes, and with a high and glittering mitre on its head. The remainder of the procession were following these two figures at a respectful distance.

The leading figure ascended the steps and took his place on the throne, whilst the lesser figure stood at the right of the throne.

The music ceased, and four men dressed in long robes advanced carrying what looked like a large cushion with a glittering object in its centre. They ascended the steps and laid the cushion and glittering object at the feet of the figure on the throne. After prostrating themselves three times, they retired backwards to the body of the platform.

Next, the figure beside the throne took what appeared to be a roll which he had been carrying, and apparently began to read from it. He then raised his left hand above his head, and those on the platform prostrated themselves once. He next lowered his hand and picked up the glittering object from the cushion, which Brian now felt sure was a crown. Holding this in both hands, he evidently began to make a speech, during which he raised the crown higher and higher, and at the same time moved it towards the head of the figure on the throne, but Brian could see no more of the scene as something had happened to his glasses. He removed them from his eyes to see what had gone wrong, but found that everything had gone dark, and that the sun had disappeared.[1]

---

[1] Zech. 14: 6-7.

He had been lying down, but got to his feet in surprise
and fear, and as he did so the earth began to tremble. The
first tremors were slight, but in a few seconds the earth was
shuddering and shaking, so that he could not keep his feet,
but fell on his face and tried to grip the shuddering earth
with scratching fingers.[1]

Instead of abating, the shaking and shuddering increased,
and from the direction of Jerusalem he could hear a sound as
of falling masonry, and an even louder cracking and groaning
of the earth's surface in the direction of the Mount of Olives;
followed by a thunder-like crash, and he felt the earth under
him heave up and fall back, after which he lost consciousness.

When he recovered consciousness the earth had become quiet,
but the sun still remained invisible, whilst there was only a
half light, which caused him to consider that it must be after
sunset. He looked at his watch, which was a shock-proof one
and which he found was still running, and saw that it was only
a few minutes after noon.

Brian lay there for some minutes listening, but everything
was silent, and he realized that the sound of distant gunfire
had ceased for the first time since the previous evening.

He rose to his feet, but found that he was dizzy and weak,
so made his way through the half light to the house of
Haggai, which he found to be a mass of ruins. He poked
amongst the débris, but could find no sign of any bodies, and
then remembered that Haggai had said that he and his friends
would remain in hiding away from the buildings during the
daylight hours, but would return after darkness fell.

He was undecided what to do, so made an appreciation of
the situation and concluded that the damage to Jerusalem
and to Gog's armoured vehicles and transport, as well as to
his personnel, must have been terrific: consequently he would
be unnoticed if he visited the city during the confusion. Further, he might there obtain means of communication with

---

[1] Ezek. 38: 19-20.

"Intelligence" at headquarters, and send in a short report of what had occurred.

He therefore set off for Jerusalem, and with little difficulty found the road which he had traversed the previous afternoon. He followed the road downhill for some distance until it began to level off, so considered that he must be near the Valley of Hinnom. Soon he noticed an acrid smell which made breathing difficult, and thinking that Gog might have had poison gas containers in his transport which had been damaged in the earthquake, thus allowing the gas to escape, he decided to go no farther downhill where the gas would be more dense.

He therefore retreated up the hill until he could no longer notice the acrid smell, and as a light breeze had sprung up from the south, considered that any gas which might be lying in the valley below would soon be dispersed towards the north. There he sat down close to the road and decided to wait until someone came along, or until it became sufficiently light to see if gas were present in the valley.

After a wait of over an hour, he heard voices whose owners appeared to be approaching up the hill. As they got closer, he could hear them talking in Hebrew, and could soon make out the figures of two men about one hundred yards down the road from where he was lying.

As the approaching men appeared to be unarmed, Brian rose to his feet and moved on to the road to meet them. On seeing him they halted, so he addressed them in Hebrew, saying that he was a stranger and asked if this was the road to Jerusalem. To this they replied in the affirmative.

His use of Hebrew seemed to reassure them, so he asked whether they knew his friend Amos Ben Jacob, and whether he was in Jerusalem.

The taller of the two men, who appeared to be the spokesman, answered that Amos was also a friend of his, but he regretted that Amos had left the city the previous day, and he could not say where he was at present.

Having discovered a mutual friend in Amos, Brian asked what had occurred in Jerusalem, and was told that Gog was to have been crowned as "Sovereign Lord of All the World," but just as the crown was being lowered on to his head, a sudden darkness had come on and a terrible earthquake had taken place, which had caused Gog's throne, with its occupant and the High Priest who was standing beside him, to collapse, and neither had since been seen. The earthquake had completely demolished the "Dome of the Rock" and other Mohammedan mosques, as well as practically all the buildings in Jerusalem.

At the same time, the Mount of Olives had split from east to west, thus forming a great valley, and many of the Jews who had been present at the attempted crowning of Gog had, as soon as they were able to get to their feet after the earthquake, in their terror lost their way in the darkness, and had fled down the valley.[1]

A great proportion of Gog's armoured fighting vehicles and transport which had been inside the city had been covered by falling buildings, and such of Gog's forces as had also been in the city and who had escaped death from falling masonry, had fled into the country.

A terrible storm, with thunder, lightning, and an unusual fire which smelt like burning sulphur, had taken place just after the earthquake,[2] and had apparently formed some kind of a gas, which had settled in the low ground along the Valley of Jehoshaphat on the east of the city, in the Valley of Hinnom to the south, and had spread up the Valley of Gihon on the west. The result was that such of Gog's forces as had encamped on these three sides of Jerusalem were killed by the gas, whilst those of his troops who had fled from the high ground of the city into the country on these three sides were also cut off:[3] thus only those who had fled to the north had made good their escape.

Brian was told that at the present time the city was practically deserted, and that none of Gog's forces were there,

[1] Zech. 14: 4-5.   [2] Ezek. 38:22.   [3] Zech. 14: 12.

except the dead, which were lying in all directions. Hundreds of Gog's dead were lying in the Valley of Hinnom, or rather in the small part of it which the men had been able to see owing to the half light, and through which they had passed as soon as the gas had been dispersed by the rising breeze.

Brian decided to continue on his way into Jerusalem, so thanked the men for their information, and again started down the hill. He was relieved to find no signs of gas as he reached more level ground at the foot of the hill. On reaching the Valley of Hinnom he saw hundreds of dead in the uniforms of Gog on both sides of the road, and also great numbers of them in their armoured vehicle and transport parks, which were massed closely together near the city.

He looked at one corpse to discover the symptoms of the gas poisoning, and found that the flesh had been consumed as if by flame or heat, whilst the eyes and tongue had also been shrivelled up by heat.[1] Another corpse was lying on its face beside the first corpse and, wishing to see if the symptoms were similar, he attempted to turn it over onto its back, but jumped backwards, as it burned his fingers.[2] He then noticed that the grass touching the corpses was withered and scorched, as were their uniforms.

Somewhat shaken and feeling very much alone, he continued up the hill leading into Jerusalem.

He found Jerusalem a desolation. All the buildings and walls appeared to have fallen down,[3] and corpses, principally of Gog's men, were lying everywhere. He noticed that many of the corpses of civilians showed wounds and decided that they must be those of the inhabitants who had been killed by the Magogians.

He saw no signs of life anywhere, except for one or two pariah dogs which seemed to have escaped the holocaust.

As there were many of Gog's mechanized vehicles parked in what had been the squares of the city, he searched for an undamaged vehicle of the signalling corps, hoping to find one

---

[1] Zech. 14: 12. [2] Isa. 66: 24. [3] Ezek. 38: 20.

whose wireless equipment might still be in working order. After trying several whose wireless equipment had failed, apparently from the motion of the earthquake, he at last found one which appeared to have escaped the general destruction.

After brushing up his code mentally, he tuned in on the wave-length of H.Q. "Intelligence," calling their code word which, after many repetitions, was answered.

He made a short and concise report of the situation at Jerusalem, stating that of those of Gog's forces which had been in or encamped about Jerusalem, only those who had fled northerly had got clear; that the remainder had been killed by gas or fumes of some peculiar description. He then asked for instructions, and signed off with his code word.

After waiting for some twenty minutes his code word was called, and on answering he was told to report to headquarters.

Following his instructions, he was leaving the city, but fortunately came across a motor cycle which appeared to be undamaged, and whose fuel tank was nearly full. He started it quite easily, and was soon in the open country. However, he was forced to go slowly as the half light still continued, and visibility was poor.

Brian passed many parks of Gog's armoured vehicles and transport, around each of which he saw corpses lying, but saw no signs of life. He stopped at one such park to ascertain whether Gog's men had been killed by the gas or fumes, but was surprised to find that all the corpses which he examined bore wounds, some having been shot, whilst others appeared to have been bayonetted or stabbed. On examining the scene more closely, he decided that the Magogians had been fighting amongst themselves and had killed each other.[1]

As he left Jerusalem farther behind the light became stronger, and he was able to increase his pace. Soon he saw ahead of him a band of men in civilian clothes, but who were carrying arms. Being undecided whether they were friend or foe, he halted, when suddenly from behind a hedge on his

---

[1] Zech. 14: 13.

right, a voice told him in Hebrew to put his hands up. Looking to see who was the owner of the voice, he discovered that he was covered by two men with rifles.

One of them advanced whilst the other kept him covered, and he was asked who he was and what he was doing. He explained that he was a Jew escaping from Jerusalem, and was then asked whether he was a Zionist, to which he replied in the negative.

This appeared to satisfy his captor, as he relaxed and called his companion, telling him to remain where he was whilst he took Brian to their leader.

On reaching the band of men, he was taken before the leader who examined him closely. On being told that he had been staying with Amos Ben Jacob before Gog took Jerusalem, the leader appeared to accept him as a friend. He told Brian that his band was one of many bands of Jews who were opposed to the Zionists, and which bands had been formed from refugees from Jerusalem and the surrounding country as soon as it had become apparent that Gog was in such strength that the city must fall.

As soon as the earthquake had occurred, their spies had seen the effect on Gog's troops, for whom they had been acting as servants, and the spies had at once fled to their own bands. The latter immediately set out to ambush the various small bodies of Magogian troops which had been scattered in their flight from Jerusalem, but had found that in practically all cases the Magogians had for some unknown reason been fighting amongst themselves, and that very few were left alive. Such as they had found alive, they had sent to join their comrades.

The leader said that they had already been in communication with three other bands of their men, all of whom had the same tale to tell.

Brian asked if he might continue his journey, to which the leader agreed, first giving him a note on which had been stamped the crest of the commander of the Jewish guerillas, and which he was told to use as a passport should be meet other similar bands.

After continuing his journey for some miles, Brian ran into a British patrol of mobile troops, to the leader of which he showed his credentials and asked to be directed to Army Head-quarters, which he reached without further incident.

CHAPTER VII.

"Armageddon." (Rev. 16: 16.)

On arrival at Army Headquarters, which he found were in the cellars of some ruined buildings, Brian went at once to "Intelligence" to report to Col. Smythe, whom he found to be very quiet and distrait.

Brian commenced to make a detailed report, but Smythe said, "Does it really matter now?" Brian was most surprised and annoyed, replying, "Why not? Won't my information be of use to you in the campaign against Gog's main forces?"

Smythe replied, "Haven't you heard? Gog has no main forces nor anything else now."

"What do you mean?" said Brian.

Smythe then told him shortly how on the previous evening just before sunset, Gog's bombers in myriads had commenced bombing our positions. This bombardment had been followed by an exceptionally heavy and accurate artillery bombardment, which lasted all night. At dawn the bombers had resumed their task, whilst the artillery fire had been redoubled.

Soon after dawn the enemy had attacked with large concentrations of tanks across the Plains of Megiddo, which attack had penetrated our lines in three places.

Our own armour had counter-attacked and driven the enemy clear of our positions, but at heavy cost to ourselves, Gog having been absolutely reckless in his use of his armour, and having paid no attention to the number which were destroyed.

The enemy had continued his attacks all morning with waves after waves of tanks, whilst, as he had complete air supremacy, his bombers had caused us heavy casualties as well as having worked great havoc to our prepared defences. His artillery had also put down fierce barrages on our positions, and had not lifted them until his tanks were on top of our front line, evidently preferring to chance hitting his own armour rather than to allow our anti-tank weapons to open fire.

They had penetrated our positions time after time, but had been driven out by our armoured local reserves, until the latter had practically all been put out of action.

Finally they had crumpled up our right flank, driving it back towards our centre, and almost at the same time had penetrated our left centre, cutting off the majority of our forces from Haifa and a possible withdrawal.

A counter-attack to restore our right flank had been launched by our general reserve, as the reserve had been concentrated in rear of the outer flank in order to cover a withdrawal on Haifa, should such become necessary.

This counter-attack had been to a certain extent successful, and had restored most of our original line, but the penetration of our left centre had continued, and the enemy had poured large concentrations of armour through the gap, which concentrations had enveloped the flanks thus formed, and had attacked them from the rear.

Gog had also sent large mobile forces around our restored right flank, his concentrations being tremendous and his reinforcements unending, and these mobile forces had again enveloped that flank.

The situation had seemed hopeless, and as Gog neither gave nor asked for quarter, it had appeared as though the British Army would be wiped out to a man, particularly as the hostile bombers had still kept up their bombing, as had the enemy artillery their heavy bombardment.

The G.O.C. had called his Staff together just before noon, and had addressed them, saying, "Gentlemen, humanly speaking, the situation is hopeless. As those who were at Dunkirk will well remember, the situation there was also hopeless so far as our own efforts were concerned, but we were saved out of it, I firmly believe, by the Hand of God. I am sure that there were very few at Dunkirk who did not pray either openly or silently. I know that I did. Gentlemen, for the first time in my life, I am going to lead you in prayer."

Very simply he had prayed for help, stating that God had saved the Army at Dunkirk, and that His Hand was not short-ened that it could not save[1] the Army in what now appeared to be a hopeless situation. He thanked God for His Mercy at Dunkirk and throughout that war, and humbly asked for similar mercy in the present situation.

As he finished, the Staff remained silent, whilst Smythe had heard a clock strike noon.

Within a few seconds the earth had begun to tremble far more than it had been doing from the detonations of the battle, and several members of the Staff had rushed to the windows to see the cause, but nothing unusual could be seen.[2]

The tremors had continued to increase greatly, and the G.O.C. had ordered everyone outside from fear of the build-ing collapsing.

On arriving in the open air, dark clouds had been seen rushing through the sky from the direction of Jerusalem, whilst the shuddering of the earth had become still more severe.

Smythe had noticed that the sounds of battle had decreased, and as he listened they died away almost altogether.

By this time the shaking of the earth had become so great that it had been impossible to keep one's feet, and the Staff had been forced to lie down on the ground, whilst a few seconds later the headquarters buildings had collapsed with a great crash.

The shaking lasted for several minutes; then ended in a final great heave upwards, after which the earth seemed to settle back into place. The sounds of battle had completely ceased, and even the birds were quiet in the ominous silence, whilst a peculiar half light prevailed.

The black clouds which had been rushing towards the Plains

[1] Isa. 59: 1.   [2] Isa. 65: 24.

of Megiddo, some miles to the north of the Headquarters, had by now arrived over the battlefield, and lightning was flashing in all directions, followed a few seconds later by tremendous thunderclaps.

Whilst the Staff had watched in silent awe, the clouds had seemed to pour fire on the earth, whilst a yellowish smoke ascended from the battlefield. The G.O.C. had borrowed a pair of field glasses which one of the Staff happened to have slung over his shoulder, and after a few seconds of observation had stated that he must see what was happening to his men.

Ordering his B.G.S. and Smythe to accompany him, the G.O.C. had entered the tank which he always used, and had the driver start for our defensive position.

When they had arrived within a couple of miles of the front line, they had seen large masses of hostile tanks approaching from the east and from the west.

Taking cover from view, they had watched the hostile tanks approach each other. The tanks moving from the east had apparently sighted those from the west first, and had opened fire on them. Those from the west had returned their fire, and having changed their direction, charged towards those from the east. The latter adopted similar tactics, and the two forces had met head on. The fight had continued until the force from the east had been wiped out, but leaving only two tanks from the western force, who in their bewilderment attacked each other,[1] with the result that one of them was put out of action, whilst the other limped back towards the battlefield in a badly damaged condition.

The G.O.C.'s tank had then continued on towards the front, passing several other concentrations of hostile tanks, all of which had apparently fought with and destroyed each other.[2] These had evidently been the armoured concentrations which the Magogians had used in the enveloping movement around our right flank, and which had encountered those who had been poured through the gap in our left centre, who, having

1 Ezek. 38: 21.   2 Zech. 14: 13.

mistaken each other for British armour, had destroyed themselves.

The G.O.C. had called on the Headquarters of the Division in whose sector they had arrived, and having picked up the Divisional Commander, had continued on to the trench system.

There, to his great relief and incredible as it may seem, he had found that the clouds had poured their message of death on Gog's forces only, and that our positions had been entirely untouched.

However, the earthquake, followed so quickly by the terrible storm with its lightning, thunder, and sulphurous fires, had completely unnerved our Officers and men, who had still been very dazed when the G.O.C. arrived. By this time the storm had ceased, but the sun had remained obscured.

The G.O.C. had then questioned the Commanding Officer of the unit on whose front they had arrived. The latter had stated that at the moment that the earthquake had commenced the enemy were pressing home a strong tank attack. The earth tremors had appeared to have affected the tracks of the tanks in some way, and they had seemed unable to grip the ground, but simply revolved with little forward movement, with the result that the attack had been stalled.

The earthquake had caused his own trenches, although well-built with "headers and stretchers," to cave in, with the result that his men had been forced to leave their trenches and take up positions in rear of the parados.

As soon as the earthquake had ceased, the clouds had commenced to belch forth fire on the enemy, as well as lightning and huge hailstones[1] of which he had been able to point out several still lying within a few yards of the parapet.

The hail had had little, if any, effect on the enemy armour, but the waves of infantry following in rear of the tanks had been bowled over like ninepins, whilst those who had escaped being hit by it had turned and run, firing on the men in the following waves. A general melee had ensued amongst Gog's

[1] Ezek. 38: 22.

infantry, during which the hail, fire, and lightning had continued to fall amongst them. The result had been that very
few of the infantry had escaped, and those who had done so
had scattered in all directions in their flight.

On the other hand, whilst the hail had had little effect on
the hostile armour, the fire which had been poured upon 'them
had ignited their fuel tanks, causing explosions. Many had
also been hit by lightning, which had fused their machinery
and had in many cases detonated their ammunition and ignited
their fuel. In fact, the plain in front of position as far as the
eye could see, had been covered with smashed and burnt out
tanks, many of which were still fiercely burning.

The G.O.C. had immediately returned to the Divisional Headquarters of the sector, where he had got into touch with the
other sectors of the front, from all of which he had received
the same story of the destruction of Gog's forces, which appeared to be complete. He had then issued orders for our
mobile troops to pursue and destroy the remnants of Gog's
forces, before they could reform into some semblance of order.
It was one of these mobile patrols which Brian had encountered on his way to Headquarters.

On their return to Army Headquarters, the G.O.C. had at
once sent for the Director of Medical Services, and had ordered
him to arrange for permanent burial parties to search the
surrounding country for the purpose of finding and burying
Gog's scattered dead.[1]

He had then told his Staff that he intended to write his
report on the battle, and did not wish to be disturbed except
for important matters. It was shortly after this order had
been given that Brian had arrived upon the scene.

Brian suggested that perhaps the G.O.C. might wish to
incorporate in his report the events which had occurred at
Jerusalem. Smythe said that if he wished to take the respon-
sibility of disturbing him, that he was free to do so, and pointed

---

[1] Ezek. 39: 12.

out the mechanized vehicle which the G.O.C. was now using as a temporary office.

He found that the G.O.C. would see him, as he wished for a report on the situation in Jerusalem, which Brian was able to give him.

When Brian had finished his report, the G.O.C. said, "All the events have been exactly in accordance with the prophecies given us in the Bible, and which I have been studying very closely lately."

"Do you realize," he continued, "that all the prophecies of these events refer to a Divine deliverance of the actual nation Israel? As we, the British, are the ones who have been delivered, it implies most forcibly that we must be Israel. Do you see the logic of this?"

"Yes, Sir," Brian replied. "I was told recently in London by my cousin who has studied the matter closely, that the Anglo-Saxon-Celtic race are Israel, and that the English are the Tribe of Ephraim, the leading tribe of the supposedly 'lost' Ten Tribes. He also told me that Gog would be destroyed by Jehovah and, as a result of that deliverance, that Israel would know that Jehovah was her God, and that she would at last realize her identity.[1] This, Sir, you have just corroborated."

The G.O.C. was most interested and asked for further particulars, which Brian gave him, also stating that Jesus was Jehovah of Hosts according to his cousin's belief, but that he himself was not yet convinced of this in his own mind.

The G.O.C. replied, "Everything points to the fact that Our Lord Jesus Christ should now return very soon, if not immediately, according to the prophecies. I believe that I shall have to incorporate in my report that it was just at the end of an Intercession for Divine help that the Army was delivered, and further that I shall have to point out in some way that events have proved to me that we are Israel, although to do so in an official report will undoubtedly be unprecedented.

---

[1] Ezek. 89: 22.

Still, Drake did it after the defeat of the Spanish Armada, I now remember, so I shall follow his example."

Saying that he must complete his report, he dismissed Brian after thanking him for his information.

Brian sought out Smythe, who still seemed very far away in thought, and told him shortly to what conclusions the G.O.C. had come. Smythe said that it was all beyond him, and asked Brian for his views; whereupon Brian told him shortly some of the information which he had been given by his cousin.

Smythe said that he had never been interested in religion and knew nothing about it, but that certainly the Army had been delivered by supernatural means, and that immediately after prayer for Divine Help; although unless he had himself seen it he never would have believed it. As it was, he did not know where he stood.

Soon they visited an improvised Mess in the cellars of one of the collapsed Headquarters buildings, where they had a somewhat scanty dinner amongst a very silent and thoughtful Staff.

After dinner they left the Mess, and found that the sky had cleared but that darkness was falling rapidly.

They strolled up and down, immersed in thought, whilst Smythe asked Brian many questions on the facts which Samuel had told him. As they strolled, Brian noticed that it was growing lighter, but unconsciously attributed it to moonrise.

Suddenly Smythe exclaimed, "What is that?" pointing to the sky in the direction of Jerusaleum.

Brian looked to where Smythe was pointing, and saw a fiery light high in the sky, which looked like a constellation of many stars, and which was shining brightly, and lighting up the whole countryside.

"What is it?" Smythe repeated.

"It looks to me like an X P," said Brian. "What do you make of it?"

"Yes," said Smythe, "it is an 'X' and a 'P.' But what does it mean?"

"I haven't the least idea," Brian replied.

In their strolling they had again approached the Head-quarters' Mess, and could hear the excited remarks of the Mess waiters and cooks, all of whom had apparently come out to look at the peculiar phenomenon.

Several other members of the Staff soon joined them, and all expressed their wonder and bewilderment at the sign.

Someone had advised the G.O.C. of the unusual constellation, and he had joined the group.

One of the senior Staff officers said to him, "What do you make of it, Sir?"

"Some years ago," he replied, "I read a book, 'The Cross of Constantine,' by J. M. Neale, and founded on the authorities of Eusebius, 'Vit-Const.' and Fleury, which described the Cross which appeared in the sky to the Christian Emperor Constantine just before his battle with Maxentius, representing the pagan forces of Rome, and which Cross was accompanied by fiery letters stating, 'By this conquer.' The book stated that the sign consisted of the Greek letters 'X' 'P', that is 'Ch' and 'r', and this abbreviation was often employed by early Christians to signify Christ. It may be said that Constantine completely defeated Maxentius and destroyed his forces."

"Our Lord Jesus Christ stated that immediately after the great tribulation, and just before His Return, that the 'Sign of the Son of Man' would appear in Heaven.[1] This peculiar constellation certainly appears to be an 'XP', and consequently I take it to be the promised 'Sign of the Son of Man,' meaning that He will return almost immediately. Gentlemen, are you ready for Him? Think it over."

Saying that he did not wish to be disturbed, the G.O.C. left the group and went to his quarters.

Smythe had arranged for blankets and sleeping accommo-

---

[1] Matt. 24: 30.

dation for Brian, and just as the latter was about to retire, he was instructed to report to the G.O.C.

On reporting, the G.O.C. told him that his report was completed and that he was sending copies by three different routes to the War Office, of which he wished Brian to deliver one copy. He stated that he had ordered a plane to be ready at dawn to fly Brian to England, and told him to make his necessary arrangements forthwith. He thanked Brian for his services whilst he had been with his Command, and stated that as the need for those services had now ended, he was to report to his own Chief after delivering the report.

He then became less official in his manner, and said, "Do you agree with me that this phenomenon must be the promised 'Sign of the Son of Man'?"

"I cannot say, Sir," Brian replied, "but as both my cousin and you yourself believe that the deliverance, which terminated what since 1939 has been practically one great tribulation, was to be followed shortly by Christ's return, and if you are both correct in this interpretation, then it would be logical to conclude that this unusual phenomenon is the 'Sign of the Son of Man,' which you both state was also promised at this time."

The G.O.C. replied, "Then you yourself are not convinced that the beliefs which both your cousin and I hold are true?" To this Brian admitted that he found it very difficult to believe in the supernatural, although he found it even more difficult to believe that the earthquake which had kept Gog from being crowned at Jerusalem, and also the destruction of Gog's forces immediately after a prayer for Divine help and also a National Day of Repentance and Prayer appointed by H. M. the King, could be coincidences only, but that he would have to think the matter over carefully before he knew exactly where he stood.

The G.O.C. said that Brian was very stiff-necked, like the ancient Israelites, and that he personally was very thankful for the fact that His Majesty the King had called the National Day of Repentance and Intercession,[1] and also was most thankful to Almighty God for His deliverance. He further stated that he himself intended to call a Day of Repentance and Thanksgiving for the Army, and would have a loud-speaker system set up by which he could address his troops, telling them of the prophecies which had been fulfilled, and of the prophecies of what events were to follow shortly, as well as what he considered the new constellation to portend, as he did not wish his men to be caught napping by the Lord's return.

"How terribly wrong these Modernist ecclesiastics have been," he concluded. "Quite recently I read of the official decision of the leaders of the Church of England and of the United Church, to the effect that we can no longer expect Christ's return in the flesh, but a spiritual return only. Now, we are having all the prophecies fulfilled as to the signs preceding His Return, and due to these false teachings, the public are absolutely unprepared."

"However," he continued, "St. Paul prophesied, 'That day shall not come, except there come a falling away first';[2] the word 'apostasy' being here translated as 'falling away,' so that we can see that the present day falling away from the Divine Truth of God's Word by the ecclesiastical church was prophesied. Further, Our Lord Himself said, 'Nevertheless when the Son of Man cometh, shall He find THE faith on the earth?'[3] The Greek states 'the faith,' but the translators have omitted the word 'the' in the English, although it should have been left in."

He then shook hands with Brian, again thanking him for his help, and after saying that he hoped that Brian would open his mind to the facts of what had occurred, he bid him good-bye.

Brian returned to his make-shift bed, and after a restless night, arose unrefreshed an hour before dawn. On leaving his quarters he found that the strange constellation was still shining

---

[1] Ezek. 36: 37.   [2] II Thes. 2: 3.   [3] Luke 18: 8.

brightly, which for some reason made him feel disturbed and depressed.

After a hasty breakfast he proceeded to the airfield where he found that the plane by which he was to travel was already warming up. He took his seat and soon the pilot opened the throttle and the plane sped across the field and rose into the air.

One motor suddenly began to run unevenly, and when the machine had attained a height of about a hundred feet, stopped altogether. The plane began to sideslip, and the pilot tried to pull it out, but his efforts were unsuccessful, and Brian saw that a crash was inevitable. He tried to save himself as much as possible, but he had omitted to fasten his safety belt, and as he heard the splintering of the wing of the plane, he was thrown sideways. His head struck a metal object, causing him to see bursts of flame, and with a roaring in his ears, he lost consciousness.

The ground crew rushed out to save the pilot and his passenger, but, as the pilot had switched off the ignition, there was fortunately no fire with which to contend.

The crew soon rescued the pilot, who had escaped injury except for a broken left arm. They then took Brian in an unconscious condition from the wrecked plane and, as an ambulance had by now arrived on the scene, rushed them off to the nearest Military Hospital.

Here the Medical Officer discovered that Brian's skull was fractured, and considered that his recovery would be slow, with the possibility that the unconscious condition might continue for days or even weeks.

The Medical Officer was correct in his diagnosis, and Brian remained unconscious for several weeks, thus being unaware of the wonderful events which were taking place, and in which he had no part.

CHAPTER VIII.

THE KING RETURNS.

One afternoon Brian finally opened his eyes and saw a nurse standing nearby. He made a slight noise which the nurse heard, and came over to look at him.

"Where am I?" he said weakly.

She told him that he had had an accident and was in hospital, but that he must not talk, and then hurried away to find the Medical Officer.

The latter soon arrived, and after examining the patient said, "You are coming along well, but you must keep quiet and not talk."

He gave Brian a sedative, and soon he drifted off into a dreamless sleep.

Next morning he awoke feeling stronger, and was given some nourishment, after which he again fell asleep.

After several days, he commenced to regain a little strength, and was allowed to say a few words, as well as being told of the plane crash, and that Col. Smythe had come to the hospital to take charge of his official documents and personal effects. He was also told that the G.O.C. had sent one of his Aides almost daily during the first part of his stay in hospital, to enquire as to his condition.

He had felt a great deal of curiosity as to the after-effects of Armageddon, and as to what further events had occurred, but the Medical Officer had given strict orders that he was not to be allowed to become excited, so his curiosity was not satisfied.

However, after a week of continual improvement, Col. Smythe was allowed to visit him one afternoon, and gave him a short account of the events after Armageddon.

He told Brian that on receipt of the G.O.C.'s full report on the events at Armageddon and at Jerusalem, His Majesty the

King had at once appointed a Day of Thanksgiving and Repentance, and had broadcast to the nations of the British Commonwealth the fact that they were Israel, as were the United States
of America, and some of the Scandinavian countries. He stated
that this fact had been known to the Royal Family since the
days of Queen Victoria. He had personally called upon every
individual of the Commonwealth to give thanks for our deliverance, and to ask God to again set up His Kingdom in Israel
under His Divine Laws.

Smythe said that from what he had seen in the Headquarters
Staff and in the Army, he believed that a "new heart" had been
given to Israel,[1] and that a new nation had been born.[2] The
change appeared to have been caused by the events at Armageddon and at Jerusalem, and particularly by the fact that
fire had fallen AMONGST the Israel nations at the same time
that it had fallen UPON Gog's forces.

This fire had fallen AMONGST Israel,[3] picking out and
destroying all the "synagogue of Satan,"[4] as well as those who
had been holding Nazi, Fascist, or Communistic ideals, and
who had caused tremendous sabotage to the Israel war effort
as soon as Gog had commenced his attack.[5]

The fire had also destroyed all the cruel and all who had still
made a practice of vice,[6] as well as those who rejoiced in the
pride of their scholarship, and had taught that the Bible was
not true.[7] Those who won lawsuits by legal trickery and not
by justice on the merits of the case had also been destroyed,[8]
with the result that Israel had seen the error into which they
had been led by Evolution, Higher Criticism, Modernism, and the
other "isms" which had been conceived by the "synagogue of
Satan" for the purpose of destroying Israel's faith in her God.

When Israel had seen the truth of God's Word, her national
trait of sportsmanship had caused her to immediately repent
whole-heartedly on a national basis, and she had honestly wished
to serve her God. His Majesty's broadcast had made Israel
adopt the attitude, "Lo: This is Our God; we have waited for

---

[1] Ezek. 11: 19; 36: 26. [2] Isa. 66: 8. [3] Matt. 13: 37-42; Ezek. 39: 6. [4] II Thes. 2: 8.
[5] Rev. 14, 9, 10. [6] Mal. 4: 1 (Fenton trans.) [7] Zeph. 3: 11. [8] Isa. 29: 21 (Fenton
trans) ; Protocol No. 8.

Him, and He will save us: This is Jehovah; we have waited for
Him, we will be glad and rejoice in His Salvation;"[1] and the
whole nation had apparently prayed earnestly that God would
again set up His Kingdom in Israel.

On the other hand, this same fire had fallen ON Magog[2] and
the other countries who had joined Gog, and had almost completely destroyed the younger generation, who had been raised
by their governments to be anti-God, and to fight against His
Word. These, as prophesied, had made war against the Lamb
and had been overcome[3] by the fire which proceeded out of His
Mouth.[4] The leaders in these countries, and all who had taken
a willing part against God and Israel, had also been destroyed.

Smythe said that the strange constellation, which all had
finally concluded must be the "Sign of the Son of Man," and
which had been visible at night throughout the whole world, had
had a most peculiar effect upon the various nations.

To Israel after her change of heart, it had seemed a sign of
promise and of great hope for the future. Great had been the
searching of Bibles, and particularly of the prophecies, for the
promised blessings on Israel, and all were waiting expectantly
for the return of Our Lord Jesus Christ, whom many now said
was Jehovah of Hosts.

It had been impossible to ascertain the opinions of the Higher
Critical and Modernistic ecclesiastics on these matters, as none
of them could be found. Smythe said that he was confident that
he had met two of them, who had formerly been chaplains, but
they were both in working clothes and insisted that they were,
and always had been, farmers and cattle-herders.[5]

On the other hand, it was reported by newspaper corre-
spondents that the nations of Continental Europe, South
America, and other non-Israel countries had been terrified by
the "sign," and had been weeping and wailing in terror.[6] The
priests of these nations had appeared to be dazed, and many
of them were even more terror-stricken than were their congregations. However, amongst these nations were a few indi-

---

[1] Isa. 25: 9. [2] Ezek. 39: 6. [3] Rev. 17: 14. [4] II Esdras 13: 10, 38. [5] Zech. 13: 5.
[6] Matt. 24: 30.

viduals who believed in the Word of God rather than in ecclesiasticism, and these had explained to the people the meaning of the "sign," and had told them of the promise that "Whosoever shall call upon the Name of Jehovah shall be saved;"[1] with the result that many had accepted Jesus as Lord and Saviour before He returned visibly.

Israel had continued to make her "enquiry" as prophesied,[2] with the result that God had sent His Son Jesus Christ to set up again the Kingdom of God in Israel, as promised.

Smythe was very reticent about the details, simply saying that there had been the sound of a great trumpet,[3] following which the Lord had appeared from the east as suddenly as lightning,[4] seated on a cloud with power and great glory,[5] and accompanied by an innumerable host of angels and saints.[6] He stated that the sight was so sudden, dazzling, and overpowering, that he had fallen on his face, feeling dizzy and ill, and could remember no details.

Smythe further stated that all who had died during Old Testament days trusting in Him as their "Redeemer, the Lord of Hosts,"[7] and those who had died in New Testament days trusting in Him as Jesus their Saviour, had been raised from the dead, and had joined the Lord in the air,[8] whilst those who were still living, and who had believed in His promises and had accepted Him as Saviour, had had their mortal bodies changed to spiritual bodies in the twinkling of an eye, and had also been caught up to join the Lord.[9]

He stated that the G.O.C. and one other member of the Staff had been amongst those who had received the spiritual body and had been caught up, and that there had been great sadness amongst the remainder of the Staff at their neglect of Bible study, but of having accepted instead the teachings of the Modernists on the subject prior to Armageddon.

The inhabitants of Jerusalem had been rebuilding the city, and had put up a temporary tabernacle on Mount Moriah, the site of the former Temple, as the Mohammedan mosques which

---

[1] Joel 2: 32. [2] Ezek. 36: 37. [3] Matt. 24: 31. [4] Matt. 24: 27. [5] Matt. 24: 30. [6] Zech. 14: 5. [7] Isa. 41: 14, etc. [8] I Cor. 15: 52; I Thes. 4: 17. [9] I Thes. 4: 16-17.

had been situated there had been completely destroyed by the earthquake.

The earthquake had caused many more changes than Brian had been able to see in the half light, as the mountains around Jerusalem had been thrown down[1] and had been flattened out, whilst the "fault" in the earth which had been used to cause the earthquake,* had formed a valley which had been filled by a deep river which ran from Jerusalem to the Mediterranean Sea, thus making Jerusalem a seaport,[2] whilst a second river flowed from Jerusalem into the Dead Sea.[3]

Still again, a river of pure water had flowed from Mount Gerizim in Galilee into the Dead Sea, thus cleansing it. When the depression in which lay the Dead Sea had become filled, the overflow formed another river flowing towards the east across the desert, and became a tributary of the Euphrates.[4] The land around these two rivers was already becoming very productive, and their waters were making "the desert blossom as a rose."[5] These rivers were called the "Rivers of the Sanctuary,"[6] as the Lord had ordered that the new Sanctuary Temple be built on Mount Gerezim (the Mount of Blessing),[7] from whose site the waters flowed.[8]

Smythe stated that the Lord had again assumed the Kingship at the request of Israel, who very much regretted the rejection of Jehovah as King by their forefathers.[9] The King had taken the name, "The Lord Our Righteousness,"[10] which Israel had gladly called Him and, as King David had been raised up he became the Prince,[11] whilst such of His descendants as had obeyed the Commandments of God and (or) accepted the Righteousness of God in Our Lord Jesus Christ, became princes also, and were given a grant of land on each side of the Sacred Grant for the Sanctuary Temple.[12]

The King had again set up His Capital at Jerusalem, and had then issued orders that the Law of the Lord, which He had given

---

[1] Ezek. 38: 20.   [2] Zech. 14: 8.   [3] Ezek. 47: 8.   [4] Ezek. 47: 8-9 (Fenton trans.)   [5] Isa. 35: 1.   [6] Ezek. 47: 12 (Fenton trans.)   [7] Deut. 11: 29.   [8] Ezek. 47: 12.   [9] I Sam. 10: 19.   [10] Jer. 23: 6.   [11] Ezek. 34: 24.   [12] Ezek. 48: 21.   * Geologists are unanimous in stating that the greatest known Geological "fault" is in the Holy Land, at Jerusalem and the Mount of Olives, so that the preparations for the earthquake have already been made.

to Moses[1] be established as the Law of the Kingdom.[2] As The King had taken the name, "The Lord Our Righteousness," it had been quite apparent that the Law was not being established for the righteousness of the individual, but for blessings, prosperity, and health, all of which had been promised by Him if the Laws were kept.[3]

The Twelve Apostles judged the Twelve Tribes of Israel[4] in accordance with the Law of the Lord, as interpreted by The King in His Sermon on the Mount,[5] whilst those who had believed on Him, and had been given the spiritual body, became His Administrative Body, and administered the Kingdom. As the Apostles and Administrative Body were controlled by the Spirit of the Lord, the administration of the Kingdom was perfect, and under perfect laws.[6]

The King had made a great feast for all Israel, repeating miracles which He had performed at His First Advent; making old and mellow wine[7] as well as rich dainties to eat.[8] At this feast, He had "removed the veil veiling the Tribesmen, and the covering that covers it from all the heathen,"[9] with the result that Israel now knew which were the Israel and other "seed of the woman" nations, and also which were the "seed of the serpent" nations, or rather what were left of the latter, as most of them had been destroyed, The King having said, "For the Day of Vengeance is in Mine heart, and the year of My Redeemed (Israel) is come."[10]

At this point in his recital, Smythe was stopped by the Medical Officer who said that Brian must rest. Brian expostulated, but the Medical Officer was adamant, so Smythe was forced to promise to make another visit next day to relate further events which had occurred during Brian's unconsciousness.

On the next afternoon, Smythe again appeared, and Brian at once asked him to continue his recital.

Smythe told how The King had increased the light of the sun sevenfold,[11] but without increasing its heat. This increased sun-

---

[1] Deut. Chapters 5-7: 12-26, 28-31.   [2] Isa. 2: 3.   [3] Deut. 28: 1-15.   [4] Matt. 19: 28.
[5] Matt. Chap. 5-7.   [6] Psa. 19: 7.   [7] and [8] John 2: 3-10; Isa. 25: 6; Matt. 14: 19, etc.
[9] Isa. 25: 9 (Fenton trans.)   [10] Isa. 63: 4.   [11] Isa. 30: 26.

light had already made a great difference to the health of Israel, not only from the increased ultra-violet rays, but also because it had killed off the evil microbes which had lurked and bred in places which formerly had not been reached by any light. Further, the people were now keeping the Divine Health Laws as regards what should and what should not be eaten, with the result that health was improving greatly in the Kingdom.

The increased light had also destroyed the diseases in the soil, which had been brought on by failure to keep the Sabbatic Law for the land,[1] and which Law had been intended to give a rest to the soil, during which the good microbes could destroy the evil ones, and cleanse the soil from disease. It had also been discovered that poisonous chemical fertilizers had had a great deal to do with the poor health of the people.

The King had announced that adherence to the Health Laws and the increased sunlight would cause such abundant health that man's life would be greatly prolonged, as it had been during the early days of the Adamic race, before sin had shortened it. Hence, The King stated He would soon be able to say, "As the days of a tree are the days of My people."[2]

The increased light had also caused plants and vegetables to grow very quickly and luxuriantly, as The King had removed the curse[3] which had been put upon the ground as a punishment on Adam,[4] and by which it had brought forth thorns, thistles, and weeds. As He had also "rebuked the devourer,"[5] so that caterpillars, locusts, and other pests could no longer devour the crops, the farmer was having a very easy time of it, and could expect enormous crops.

The King had also set the price of grain at $2.42 (ten shillings approx.) per bushel (the equivalent of the price set in Lev. 27: 16), whilst other commodities took their values in accordance with the basic price of grain. Thus the farmer was assured of a good and fair price for his crops; could afford to pay good wages (which drew many city workers back to healthy country life) and had at last come back into his own.

[1] Lev. 25: 1-7, 21.   [2] Isa. 65: 22.   [3] Isa. 55: 13.   [4] Gen. 3: 17-18.   [5] Malachi 3: 11.

It had become apparent to all that the farmer's difficulties prior to the return of The King had been due entirely to the plans of International Finance.

The King had ordered that the Administrative Body issue its own currency, based on goods and work hours, and that the former government's guarantee of the chartered banks' currency be cancelled. In Canada, this had the effect of reducing the chartered banks' paper dollar to one-quarter of its value, as they had been permitted to issue $4.00 of paper money for each dollar of gold backing; whilst for each dollar of paper money, they had been permitted to issue $19.00 in credit *at interest*. (Vide official Hansard of "Standing Committee on Banking and Commerce, June, 1939, pp. 7, 102-103.) As this had meant that there was in the credit dollar a backing of only 1¼c gold, whilst the banks had been charging several times that amount in interest, it had been judged that the credit dollar was valueless, and that all loans which had been made on that basis had more than been repaid by the interest charged. All such loans had accordingly been cancelled *in toto*.

Further, as the Law of the Lord was now the Law of the Kingdom, no usury or interest (which are synonymous according to the best dictionaries), was allowed;[1] hence the banks had been forced to resume their proper role of clearing houses only, and operated on a commission basis, but with no interest.

The Kingdom had therefore gone back to the position which it held prior to 1844, at which time the ancestors of International Finance had foisted the Bank Charter Act on an unsuspecting people, and before which the charging of interest had been illegal since the time of Alfred the Great.

The King had therefore cancelled all loans on which interest was being exacted, stating that the taking of interest was an infraction of His Laws, and that the punishment for taking interest was to be the loss of the loan.

However, as one of the first acts of The King had been to announce a "Lord's Release" of all debts, as in a Sabbatic

[1] Deut. 23: 19-20.

year,[1] by which all debts which debtors had been unable to pay were cancelled, and The King Himself had taken over all the debts which had been released, and had promised that He Himself would repay in blessing and prosperity all creditors who had released such debts, the cancellation of all loans would have taken place in any case. Thus those who had made loans at interest were not unduly punished, as the great majority of them had been unaware that it was contrary to Divine Law to charge interest.

Thus Israel were able to enter the Kingdom absolutely free from any financial debts, national or individual.

Smythe said that many of the scientific and medical theories which had been taught to the people were entirely untrue, and it had been found that the "Head of the Snake" had wilfully taught these theories to adversely affect the health and mental outlook of those whom they had considered to be "Goyim" (Gentiles.) (Vide Protocol No. 2.) The originators of these methods had been destroyed by the King, but the exponents of these theories had been exposed to ridicule, and now avoided public recognition, instead of seeking it as formerly.

The King stated that He had warned His people of these pseudo-scientific theories through Isaiah, saying, "So on this Race (Israel) I lay wonders, add wonders to wonders, destroying its scientists' science, and baffling its scholars' researches;"[2] but that they had failed to take notice of His warnings.

Smythe stated that Israel were now very chastened and meek, and not at all self-satisfied any longer; in fact the prophecy, "In that day shalt thou not be ashamed for all thy doings, wherein thou hast transgressed against Me?"[3] had been truly fulfilled.

Brian had asked many questions during Smythe's recital, with the result that time had flown, and the Medical Officer once more told Smythe that he must leave.

Before leaving, Smythe told Brian that as all armies had been disbanded,[4] The King having said that He would destroy

_____
[1] Deut. 15: 1-2.   [2] Isa. 29: 14 (Fenton trans.)   [3] Zeph. 3: 11.   [4] Isa. 2: 4; Mic. 4: 3.

any nations which might attempt to attack His people in future, he had decided to return to Britain where he had a small estate, and that he had taken passage for the following morning. He therefore asked Brian to pay him a visit when the latter returned to Britain, and after wishing him a speedy recovery, said good-bye and left.

Brian remained in the hospital for several months longer, gradually regaining his strength, but found that he was still unable to move his left leg. When he had recovered sufficient strength to stand the shock, the Medical Officer told him that the accident had paralysed the leg, and that it was probable that he would never recover the use of it.

As soon as he had regained sufficient strength, Brian had written to his cousin Samuel, telling of his experiences and of the accident. To this letter he received a reply, asking him to return to Britain as soon as he was able to travel and, as "Intelligence" had been disbanded, there being no further use for its services, suggesting that Brian live with him, or at any rate stay with him until he had decided how he would employ his time.

Brian replied, stating that his leg was paralysed and that he had therefore decided to retire to the country, there to live on his pension. In the meantime, he would be very glad to stay with his cousin until he could find a suitable cottage to which to retire.

A few months later, the Medical Officer stated that he considered that Brian was sufficiently recovered to travel. Brian therefore obtained a reservation by the earliest possible sailing, and returned to Britain, where he arrived without incident.

CHAPTER IX.

The Kingdom of God on Earth.

On his arrival at Southampton, Brian was met by Samuel and, after being carefully placed in the latter's limousine, they started for London.

Samuel asked Brian to tell him of the events which had taken place in the Holy Land, and after doing so, Brian said, "If you don't mind my saying so, I am much surprised that, in view of your knowledge and beliefs, you were not given the spiritual body and made part of the Administrative Body."

"I have come to the conclusion," Samuel replied, "that it is the result of procrastination, and of thinking too much of my position in Jewry. I knew that Messiah, The King, had said that believers were to confess their faith in Him and to be baptised,[1] and this was taught by His Apostles, but I kept putting off my confession of faith and baptism, perhaps because it would affect my position in Jewry. The result was that when He returned I had not been baptised into His Body, although it was not from ignorance of what I should do. I could not therefore be made part of His Administrative Body, my neglect having been wilful from preferring my position in Jewry. Further, The King had said, 'Except ye eat the Flesh of the Son of Man, and drink His Blood, ye have no Life in you,'[2] referring to His Institution of the Last Supper, whereby by faith the believer partakes spiritually of His Body and Blood, and thus receives Spiritual and Eternal Life. This, from procrastination, I had failed to do, so by my own neglect I was deficient of spiritual life."

"As you may imagine," he continued, "I very much regret, now that it is too late, that I allowed my temporary position amongst my friends and associates to so influence me that I lost the opportunity to be chosen for the Administrative Body. Although everything in the Kingdom is already almost perfect again, since Jehovah's Natural Laws were established, and everyone is happy and contented, with nothing to fear in the

[1] Mark 16: 16; Acts 2: 38. [2] John 6: 53.

future, still the members of His Body are always so much more free and joyous in their spiritual bodies. Just think of what the spiritual body must mean to them; always able to be where they wish to be,[1] with no effort on their part; always in constant touch with The King, being perfectly controlled by His Spirit, and receiving their power from Him. Although our own mortal bodies are already becoming infinitely more healthy, and consequently our lives will be greatly prolonged, still I am sure that we cannot feel the freedom and joyousness which the members of His Body feel; which daily makes me regret my procrastination."

"I am glad," said Brian, "that you have explained the reason why you did not receive the spiritual body. I have met so many chaps in the Holy Land who appeared to be such really good men, that it puzzled me as to why they had not been also chosen for the Administrative Body."

"I am afraid that you had missed the whole point," his cousin replied, "and have been led astray by the Modernist teachings that it is man's own righteousness which fits him for the Kingdom of God. Since the fall of Eve, and through her, of Adam, man has been under the control of Satan, who by his 'Great Lie,' 'Ye shall not surely die,'[2] had caused the spiritual and then the physical death of man, as man's sin separated him from Jehovah, the source of spiritual and physical life. Satan had also by his lie usurped the dominion of the earth, which Jehovah had given to man.[3] Man could not therefore work out his own salvation, as he was continually deceived by Satan's lies, and was in a condition of 'original sin' through the fall of Adam."

"Jehovah had therefore to free man from Satan's dominion through the death and resurrection of His Son, the Son of Man, Who destroyed the power of death,[4] and thereby gave back to man the latter's lost freedom, which believers received only by accepting Jesus as Saviour prior to His return, but which He, as The King, is now giving back to all in the Kingdom."

"It is, however, the free gift of Jehovah,[5] and has nothing to

---

[1] John 20: 19, 26, etc.   [2] Gen. 3: 4.   [3] Gen. 1: 28.   [4] Heb. 2: 14.   [5] Rom. 6: 23.

do with man's own works of righteousness, which as Isaiah says, 'are as filthy rags.'[1] It therefore had to be accepted as a free gift, that is by accepting Jesus as the individual's own personal Saviour and being baptised into His Body, and also by partaking by faith of His Body and Blood in order to gain increased spiritual life, as He is the Way, the Truth, and the Life,[2] and also the Door to the Kingdom,[3] and there is no other Door."

"These chaps, whom you say were such good men, had unfortunately missed the Door it would appear, so could not be members of His Body, no matter how good they were in their own righteousness."

Brian then asked for some particulars as to what differences had been caused in Britain as a result of the setting up of the Kingdom.

In reply, Samuel explained that the elimination of interest had caused the billions held in savings banks and other non-productive investments to be reinvested in the various industries and productive enterprises. This had caused such an increase in employment that unemployment in Israel had ceased.

Brian then asked if dividends were now legal, or if they had also been eliminated. His cousin explained that dividends and interest were entirely different matters. Dividends were a share of the profits from productive enterprise, and were only paid when a profit had been made; on the other hand, interest was paid for the use of money without any productive effort, and must be paid whether a profit were made or not. Hence, if a profit were not made over a period of years, but interest must nevertheless be paid, it became confiscatory of capital.

Further, the investment of funds into productive effort caused employment. On the other hand, the investment of funds in interest-bearing investments made no jobs for workers, and hence caused unemployment.

Again, the heavy taxes formerly made upon business by the governments had caused capital to be invested in interest-bearing investments rather than in productive industry, which

---

[1] Isa. 64: 6.   [2] John 14: 6.   [3] John 10: 9.

in turn had caused unemployment. It was now apparent, Samuel said, that heavy taxes had been the basic cause of unemployment, but that International Finance had based their financial and economic theories on the premise that unemployment could not be eliminated, which theory had covered up the fact that the real basic cause was heavy taxation, caused primarily by the necessity of paying interest on the national debts to International Finance.

Under the Law of the Lord business was now flourishing. There were absolutely no taxes on it whatever, as the Tithe was exacted from the owner's or individual shareholder's share of the profits only.

As Brian already knew, The King had cancelled all taxes, and had reinstituted the Tithe as the only tax in the Kingdom. The Tithe consisted of approximately 10 per cent of the net income of the individual, after many deductions for feasts ordained by The King, and other deductions had been made. In the case of a very rich man it ran as high as 16 per cent, but the great majority of the people paid 10 per cent on net income only. As it was on the increase only, it was a natural law, and not confiscatory of capital. Succession taxes and all other direct and indirect taxes were cancelled forever.

Samuel continued that there were now no taxes whatever on dwellings, farms, nor on any other buildings, nor on land. No taxes on machinery, motor cars, tractors, nor on other such things. No taxes on tobacco, cigarettes, wine, liquor, beer, matches, nor on any other items of which he could think. No payments on licenses for motor cars, drivers' licences, radio licences, nor on any other licences.

No Customs duties on motor cars, machinery nor on anything else. No Excise taxes on liquor, wine, beer, nor on any other items. Hence the consumer was once again blessed with low prices, and which could never again be raised by heavy taxation.

The King had stated that there would never again be war, but instead continual peace and prosperity, as He would ensure

that His Laws were enforced. Hence rationing and price control
would never again be necessary, particularly as it had been
found that price control was actually an artifice of International
Finance to maintain the values of their currency above that of
the commodities and labour of the people.

"It is a wonderful thing," Samuel continued, "that the some
80,000 volumes of British Laws, most of which no one knew,
are now cancelled, and in their place are the few pages of the
Laws given us in the Bible. That was the deathblow of
bureaucracy, as now the judges are controlled by the Spirit of
The King, and they interpret His Laws in accordance with His
Will, and their judgements are His.[1] Hence these few Laws are
sufficient for all purposes of government and administration,
thus giving the citizens of the Kingdom absolute and true freedom with which no one can interfere, provided that they keep
those few Laws, the broad principles of which are embodied in
the Ten Commandments."[2]

"But," said Brian, "are there not a lot of ordinances and
religious ceremonials in the Laws?"

"Not at all," his cousin replied. "The ordinances and other
religious ceremonials were all abolished by the Atonement of
Messiah. As St. Paul tells us, Messiah nailed the ordinances to
His Cross and did away with them."[3]

"No. It is only the National Laws, as given us in Deuteronomy
principally, which are now in force, and which deal with economic
and financial matters, agriculture, health, civil administration,
and criminal matters."

"The attitude of the Administrative Body is one of service,
and with the viewpoint that the State exists for the benefit of
the individual, which is the exact opposite of the Nazi, Fascist,
and Communistic ideals that the individual exists for the benefit
of the State. This latter idea, the 'Head of the Snake' had been
insinuating into the Israel countries gradually for some years
through bureaucracy."

Brian interjected a question as to whether the Tithe would

---

[1] Deut. 1: 17.   [2] Exo. 20: 1-17.   [3] II Col. 2: 14.

not provide entirely too small a revenue for the needs of the nation.

To this Samuel replied that as the national debt had been cancelled, and there was now no interest to be paid from taxes: as everyone was becoming healthy, and hence no health insurance was required: as there was no unemployment, hence no unemployment "relief" was necessary: and particularly due to the great prosperity of those who paid the full Tithe, it had been found that the Tithe was more than sufficient to meet all the present national expenditure.

The King had stated that whoever paid the full Tithe would be greatly blessed and prospered, and had told the Nation to prove Him and see if it were not so.[1] Israel had proved Him, and had been astonished at the ensuing blessing and prosperity.

Free trade having been established between the Israel nations, there were no Excise taxes of any description, which had helped greatly in allowing the consumer low prices for all commodities.

Labour troubles had entirely ceased, due to the "new heart" given to Israel, and to the fact that there was great prosperity in all business, caused by the elimination of taxes on business operations. This had been made possible by the cancellation of all debt, as in the Sabbatic year, and the consequent elimination of the payment of interest on them had made any taxation on business entirely unnecessary. At present, owners were able and willing to pay fair and just wages, so that all had become prosperous. Labour had therefore been quite satisfied, particularly as the trouble-makers amongst union officials had been removed by The King when He had removed all trouble-makers.

No unions were now necessary, as both Capital and Labour co-operated amicably, and the Administrative Body were always ready to settle justly any disputes which might arise.

The prosperity resulting from following The King's Laws had soon caused such an increase in industry that it had been necessary to obtain workers from other countries to do the manual work, whilst Israelites were employed in executive,

---

[1] Mal. 3: 10.

managerial and other important positions only. This was The King's ruling in the matter.[1]

With the new heart of flesh which had been given to Israel,[2] all had been glad to lend to needy neighbours at the beginning of The King's regime, but soon there was such prosperity in the Kingdom that there were no poor, as promised when Israel kept the Law of the Lord.[3] Hence lending became unnecessary.

Samuel pointed out what a great difference the "new heart" had made to everyone's viewpoint. When The King had cancelled all such debts as the debtors were unable to pay, the people had accepted the ruling with gladness, and creditors had taken pleasure in forgiving the debts of their debtors. As Samuel said, "My friends and I all gladly cancelled all the debts owed to us which the debtors were unable to pay. I could not imagine myself doing this before we received the 'new heart,' nor could any of my friends with whom I discussed the matter. However, the same attitude was prevalent throughout all Israel, and everyone was glad to free their debtors."

Everyone had become so prosperous, Samuel continued, that the money incentive had almost disappeared in business, and the pleasure of giving service and adding to the public welfare was already becoming the main consideration.

The public health had so improved that many hospitals, clinics, and sanatariums had been devoted to other purposes, whilst many doctors had already turned to other fields of endeavour.

Insurance companies had liquidated their assets, as adherence to the Law of the Lord was all the insurance necessary to provide prosperity, whilst those who refused to adhere to these natural laws were not allowed insurance to protect them.

Everyone now kept the Sabbath, Samuel explained, as a day of rest and gladness. The keeping of the Sabbath was the Fourth Commandment, and prosperity was promised if it were kept.[4] However, as everyone knew the Lord, from the least of them unto the greatest of them,[5] religion was now a thing

---

[1] Isa. 14: 2; 60: 12.   [2] Ezek. 11: 19.   [3] Deut. 15: 4-5.   [4] Isa. 56: 4; 58: 13-14.   [5] Jer. 31: 34.

of spontaneity and joy, and priests no longer intoned mournfully, with other hypocrisies.

Further, it was now seen that the Christian Sunday was actually the former Seventh Day Sabbath. The King had set back the sun 23 hours and 20 minutes at Joshua's request,[1] and again a further 40 minutes when He set back the shadow on the sundial 10 degrees as a sign to Hezekiah.[2] Israel and Judah had been blinded to this change of a day, as The King had said, "Unto whom (Israel) I sware in My wrath that they should not enter into My Rest."[3] However, after He had redeemed Israel, He allowed Christians to "enter into My Rest," and the correct day was again brought into force as the "Day of Rest."

Samuel also stated that some years earlier, scientists had discovered that the pulse beats less strongly each seventh day, but in Israel's blinded condition at that time, they had not seen that the remedy was to use that day as a day of rest: the weaker pulse-beats being a sign that the seventh day rest was a natural law. He also explained that at the time of the French Revolution, the French had made every tenth day a day of rest, to conform to the Metric system, but everyone had become tired and listless, and even the mules in the mines had sickened and died, so that they had been forced to return to the natural law of a seventh day rest.

It had been apparent that The King had provided the United States of America and Canada as the countries into which those Israelites had been gathered, who had been scattered amongst the heathen nations,[4] and had not previously rejoined their own tribes in the British Isles, or in other Israel countries. Unfortunately a considerable number of "seed of the serpent" nations had also moved there, and had instituted many theories and practices which were contrary to Israel ideals. These had been some of the "tares" to which the King had referred,[5] and He had had them removed, as they had been "thorns in the sides" of Israel.[6]

---

[1] Josh. 10: 12-14 (Vide "Joshua's Long Day," by Prof. Totten.) [2] II Kings 20: 9-11.
[3] Psa. 95: 11. [4] Amos 9: 9. [5] Matt. 13: 38. [6] Num. 33: 55.

As regards Canada, when the unveiling of the Tribes of Israel had taken place,[1] the French Canadians had been much surprised to find that the great majority of them were of Norman (Tribe of Benjamin) or of Breton (Tribe of Judah) descent, and therefore brother Israelites who had been regathered into Israel. They had shown remorse at their previous anti-British attitude, which they now realized was due to the false teachings of priestcraft, from which they had been freed by the return of The King.

They had gladly accepted the British language, which The King had made the language of the Kingdom,[2] and particularly when they realized that their Norman ancestors, who had invaded Britain, had been to a large extent responsible for it.

Samuel stated that his ideas as regards the Zionist Party had been proved to be correct. There had been very few Semitic Jews amongst their leaders, the majority of them being Ashkenazim or other converts to Judaism, but who were not Semitic nor of Israel blood. It had also been evident that the "Head of the Snake" had been simply another name for the "synagogue of Satan," of whom The King had warned us,[3] and that their wish to obtain control of the Holy Land and of Jerusalem was for the purpose of there crowning their "Sovereign Lord of all the World," as they had attempted to do.

It had also been proved, Samuel continued, that it was they who had evolved all the infidel theories against the Bible, such as Higher Criticism, Modernism, Evolution, Communism, Socialism, and all other such infidel "isms," as their principal idea had been to prevent The King from setting up His Kingdom.

The "Head of the Snake" had been destroyed by the King,[4] but only after they had fulfilled His judgement on them.[5]

As regards the real Semitic Jew, it had also been found that a large proportion of them were descendants of Shelah, son of Judah by a Canaanite woman,[6] and these had been some of the "Evil Figs"[7] who had been "removed into all the Kingdoms of the earth for their hurt, to be a reproach and a proverb, a

---

[1] Isa. 25: 7 (Fenton trans.) [2] Zeph. 3: 9. [3] Rev. 2: 9, 3: 9. [4] II Thes. 2: 8. [5] Rev. 3: 9. [6] Gen. 38: 1-10. [7] Jer. 24: 8-10.

taunt and a curse, in all places whither I shall drive them." However, the King had cleansed the blood of such of them as had accepted Him, as He had promised to do.[1]

Samuel said that everyone now realized that Israel's pre-Kingdom troubles had been entirely due to neglect of the Natural Laws given in the Law of the Lord. It had been quite apparent that Satan had no power over those who kept these Natural Laws of the Lord. On the other hand, as soon as Satan was successful in tempting Israelites to disobey these Laws, he was able to gain the dominion over them, as he had of the world-system.

"Blackstone, the eminent authority on jurisprudence," said Samuel, "had warned us of this many years ago, stating, 'A command concerns, primarily, a single prescribed requirement, that is it calls for either definite action or inaction on the part of those to whom the command is directed'."

"'Consequently, disobedience to any one of the Divin Commandments throws the whole structure of national life out of harmony with universal law.'"

"Blackstone said also that the law of nature, being coeval with mankind and dictated by God Himself, is superior in obligation to any other. That it is binding throughout the world, and that no human laws have any validity if contrary to it. That all laws which are valid, derive all their force and authority from this original Law of God. That, on account of the blindness and imperfection of human reasoning, God had given a Divine and direct revelation of His Natural Laws, and that the doctrines thus delivered are called the revealed or Divine Law, and are to be found only in the Holy Scriptures."

"It is therefore apparent," said Samuel, "that our forefathers believed in the Law of the Lord before they were led astray by 'scholarship,' as taught our ecclesiastics by the 'synagogue of Satan's carefully laid plans."

"However, it would have been impossible for the Israel nations to have established the Law of the Lord, even had their govern-

---

[1] Joel 3: 21.

ments wished to do so, as the 'Head of the Snake' had gained
such control over the various governments through their 'secret
advisers,' as openly stated in their Protocol No. 2, that the
governments' hands were tied, and it required that Israel make
her 'enquiry' for Divine help before she could be freed from the
coils of the snake."

"It certainly demonstrates," he continued, "the power of
which Satan had been possessed in that Israel were completely
bound and deceived by his lies and deceits, and were yet unaware
of it. It further demonstrates the meaning of St. Paul when
he stated, 'For we wrestle not against flesh and blood, but
against principalities, against powers, against the rulers of the
darkness of this world, against spiritual wickedness in high
places,'[1] and it was quite obviously for this reason that Israel
was forced to make her 'enquiry' before she could be freed.
Jehovah had long since 'made an end of sins'[2] through the
Sacrifice of His Son, but Israel had refused to believe and accept
it nationally, so had to be made to do so by force of circumstances."

"In her hereditary stubbornness, she had fought the war
against the Nazis and Fascists, nationally trusting in her own
strength. Even victory over these nations could not free her from
Satan's enormous power. Hence it had been necessary to make
her see the impossibility of defeating Gog openly on the battlefield, and also defeating his saboteurs who had been secretly
ensconsed in all her departments of church, state, and industry,
before she would return to her God and 'enquire' of Him to do
it for her.[3] As we know now, it was as a result of the 'enquiry'
that The King set up the Kingdom, with our present blessings
of peace, prosperity, and health, and we also know that He had
been hopefully waiting for Israel to ask Him to do so."[4]

"Jehovah had given Israel freewill to serve Him or not, as
He wanted only willing citizens in His Kingdom. He knew
her stubborn heart, and Daniel had therefore been told, 'when
he shall have accomplished to scatter the power of the Holy

---

[1] Eph. 6: 12.   [2] Dan. 9: 24.   [3] Ezek. 36:37.   [4] Dan. 12: 12; Heb. 10: 13 (Fenton trans.)

People, all these things shall be finished,'[1] as He knew that it would be necessary for Him to permit Israel's power to be dispersed before she would nationally and whole-heartedly turn to Him for deliverance. However, His plan for Israel has now been carried out, and St. Paul's prophecy, 'And so all Israel shall be saved,'[2] will also be fulfilled."

The cousins had many matters about which to talk, and so the journey passed quickly. As they entered the suburbs of London, Brian asked if Samuel had had any news of Amos Ben Jacob. Samuel replied that he had corresponded with him several times in recent months. That on the destruction of Gog's forces, Amos had realized that the British, who had accepted Jesus as Messiah, had been saved by Divine intervention, whilst the Jews who had remained in Jerusalem, and who had refused to accept Him, were massacred in great numbers by Gog's forces.[3]

He had therefore studied the prophecies very carefully, and in consequence had concluded that Jesus was Messiah, Jehovah of Hosts. He had communicated his conclusions to such of the other Jewish leaders as had escaped from Jerusalem, and had expounded the prophecies to them, with the result that not only had they themselves accepted Jesus as Messiah, but had also preached this message to their followers, who had practically all accepted Him also before His Return in the flesh.

The car soon reached Samuel's home and Brian was carefully carried into Samuel's study, which he had left so many months earlier. Samuel ordered wine to be·brought, and they drank a toast to Brian's homecoming, his cousin regretting that his wife was unable to join them in the toast, as she was spending a few days with her mother.

"The miraculous provision of wine by The King,"[4] said Samuel, "at the Great Feast which He prepared on His Return, was to some of the narrow-minded sects the most astonishing act in the setting up of the Kingdom. They had absolutely closed their minds to the fact that He had made a large quantity of wine

---

[1] Dan. 12: 7.   [2] Rom. 11: 26.   [3] Zech. 14: 2.   [4] Isa. 25: 6.

at the wedding at Cana, and that it was the best wine at the wedding. As the ancient firkin was approximately nine gallons, and as there were six water-pots holding two to three firkins apiece,[1] you may calculate for yourself what the quantity was."

"Further, Messiah had said at the institution of the Last Supper, 'Verily, I say unto you, I will drink no more of the fruit of the vine, until that day that I drink it anew in the Kingdom of God;'[2] and when He fulfilled His Promise at the Great Feast, the narrow-minded had been shocked to see their pet theories completely upset by Him: as their attitude had been that of those to vhom He referred when He said, 'The Son of Man is come eating and drinking;' and you say, 'Look at Him: an eater and drinker of wine; a friend of tax-collectors and profligates.' "[3]

"These sects had tried to insist that the wine was unfermented grape juice, but as Dr. Bullinger, D.D., points out, unfermented wine is a *modern* idea, and a contradiction of terms, as to be wine it must have fermented. Further, Bullinger gives the eight names in the Scriptures which have been translated as 'wine' or 'strong drink,' and all are fermented. The most usual one used for wine is 'Yayin' from the root 'Yayan,' to ferment. In the 'wine' referred to in the Great Feast,[4] the word 'shemarim' is used, from the root 'shamar,' to keep or lay up; hence old wine, purified from the lees, and racked off."

"Again, in the Law for the use of that portion of the Tithe to be used for feasting, Israel was told, 'And thou shalt bestow that money for whatsoever thy soul lusteth after, for oxen, or for sheep, or for wine (Yayin), or for strong drink (Shekar), or for whatsoever thy soul desireth; and thou shalt eat there before the Lord Thy God, *and thou shalt rejoice,* thou and thine household.'[5] Shekar was a very intoxicating drink made from barley, honey, or dates."

"However, as in the days of the Pharisees, Satan has always led the self-righteous away from Jehovah's Truth as given in His Word, so that they would accept his ideas of what was

---

1 John 2: 3-10. 2 Mark 14: 25 (Fenton trans.) 3 Luke 7: 34 (Fenton trans.) 4 Isa. 25: 6. 5 Deut. 14: 26.

right instead of trusting in the Righteousness of God, and in this way Satan kept many from coming to God."

"The average unthinking person considered that these narrow-minded ideas were in God's Word, never realizing that they were the ideas of pharisaical men and entirely contrary to God's Word on the subject. The result was that many who had never studied God's Word did not wish to have anything to do with so-called Christianity on account of such narrow-minded and un-Biblical ideas. Now that everyone knows the King, 'from the least of them to the greatest of them,'[1] these false ideas have all been eradicated, to the amazement of the narrow-minded and self-righteous."

"I was in Canada and the United States when prohibition was in force, and had many arguments with rabid prohibitionists. In most cases they were prohibitionists on religious grounds, and when I showed them from the Scrptures that moderate drinking, but of course not drunkenness, was entirely Biblical, they would immediately explain that what they were really against was the legalized liquor traffic."

"This always amused me greatly, as it was entirely due to the activities of the 'Drys' that the liquor traffic had become what it was. Prior to their agitations, any person could make and sell liquor, wine, or beer, or buy it openly at their merchants."

"As a result of their agitations, the large liquor interests had seized the opportunity to gain control of the manufacture of alcoholic beverages, and had had laws passed whereby it became a major crime for anyone else to manufacture them. Also the governments seized the opportunity to raise taxation by bringing in government control, and raising the prices of liquor, wine, and beer to several times their former prices."

"The bootlegging and hi-jacking systems, with their murders and other crimes, were instituted as a result of the 'Dry' laws, as the great majority of reasonable people had no respect for, nor would they abide by, legislation affecting what they could drink and consequently they obtained liquor and other drinks

[1] Jeremiah 31: 34.

from bootleggers. In many cases they did not particularly want the liquor, but they refused to accept a law which was un-Biblical and unreasonable."

"We are told that drunkenness is a 'work of the flesh,' and in trying to do away with drunkenness the 'Drys' started up a series of bootlegging and hi-jacking murders and other spiritual crimes, which were far worse than the original evil which they were trying to eradicate. Perhaps the worst result of their efforts was that the contempt for the 'Dry' laws was the 'thin edge of the wedge' for contempt for all law and order by many, and in the case of the youth of the countries this was particularly noticeable."

"The Bible tells us, 'To the Law and to the Testimony: if they speak not according to this Word, it is because there is no Light in them;'[1] and Messiah is the Light.[2] We are also told, 'And lean not unto thine own understanding.'[3] The prohibitionists paid no attention to the Word, but leant on their own understanding; hence they became responsible for the bootlegging murders and other spiritual crimes, and for the great contempt for law and order which resulted."

"The name by which The King is now called, 'The Lord Our Righteousness,'[4] shows to even the most self-righteous that it is the 'Righteousness of The King which counts, not self-righteousness, and that that Righteousness is set forth in His Word, as He is the Word.' "[5]

"Further, Jehovah's free gift of His Righteousness to man was no afterthought, as we were told of, 'The Lamb slain from the foundation of the world;'[6] so that anyone who studied His Word as it is given us, could see that He had never demanded self-righteousness of man, but only faith in His Righteousness, as in the case of Abraham, the father of the faithful. It was by causing man to seek after self-righteousness, which as Isaiah tells us is 'as filthy rags,'[7] that Satan caused man to be led astray from accepting 'The Lord Our Righteousness.' When man accepted Jehovah's Righteousness, then His Spirit led man to follow

[1] Isa. 8: 20.   [2] John 8: 12.   [3] Proverbs 3: 5.   [4] Jer. 23: 6.   [5] John 1: 1 and 14.   [6] Rev. 13: 8.   [7] Isa. 64: 6.

and keep His Word for, as The King said, 'He that abideth in Me, and I in him, the same bringeth forth much fruit: FOR WITHOUT ME ye can do nothing.'[1] In other words, Satan was too strong and subtle for man, and it required the Holy Spirit to overcome Satan's lies and deceits, as human reasoning was of itself unable to discern what things were true and what things were Satan's lies.''

"No! All that had ever been demanded of man was that he accept Jehovah's Righteousness, and then try to live up to it.''

"But,'' said Brian, "what difference was there between self-righteousness and trying to live up to the Righteousness of God?''

"There was the greatest difference,'' Samuel replied. "The first was the carrying of a heavy burden to establish and maintain one's own righteousness, and which burden had always been too heavy to be borne successfully by our forefathers, due to 'original sin' through the fall of Adam. In the case of accepting Jehovah's Righteousness, this had been established and forever maintained by the Sacrifice of Messiah, and the righteousness of the believer was established forever by it, and was an accomplished fact. Trying to live up to it was therefore simply 'playing the game;' and now that they have been delivered from Satan's lies, and all know The King and His Truth, the national trait of sportsmanship of the Israel nations will cause them to do this voluntarily and freely throughout the Kingdom.''

"However, as regards the use of wine and liquor, we were warned to be moderate, as 'Drunkards shall not inherit the Kingdom of God,'[2] and that drunkenness was one of the works of the flesh.''[3]

Samuel ordered dinner to be served in the study, as Brian was forced to have his meals served on a tray.

At the beginning of the meal, Samuel said to his cousin, "Would you like some meat served with your dinner? The vegetables and fruit have so improved in taste and excellence since the sunlight increased, that we have gradually and im-

[1] John 15: 5. [2] I Cor. 6: 10. [3] Gal. 5: 21.

perceptibly been giving up the use of meat. Now we seldom think of it, although we still use fish at times, and also eggs. Many new vegetable and fruit dishes have been invented, and my friends tell me that they also have neglected meat in favor of a more vegetarian diet."

Brian replied that he found the new vegetable and fruit dishes most palatable, and felt no desire for meat, or for that matter, fish either.

Samuel explained during the meal that several of the outside nations had realized the blessings and prosperity of Israel, and had recently requested The King that they be permitted to join His Kingdom and have His Laws established. The King had gladly acceded to their request, and had sent members of His Administrative Body to explain His Laws and to establish them in the nations in question. Samuel stated that in his opinion, it would not be long before all nations would wish to join His Kingdom also, and that soon The Lord Our Righteousness would once again be King of the earth,[1] and that He would have attained this as the wish and at the request of all His citizens, now that Satan could no longer deceive them by his lies.

As Brian had had a very tiring day, he decided to retire early, so his cousin had him carried to his bedroom, accompanying him to see that he had everything that he required.

Whilst Brian was retiring, Samuel said to him, "I cannot understand why you have not been healed long ago."

"I am afraid that that is an impossibility," Brian replied. "At the hospital they had the very best medical advice, and the consensus of opinion was that my leg was permanently paralysed."

"Oh: I don't mean cured by doctors," replied his cousin. "I mean healed by one of the Health Officials of the Administrative Body. Did not the doctors at the hospital tell you that the Administrative Body had been given the power to heal, as had the Apostles after Messiah's Ascension?"

---

[1] Zech. 14: 9; Isa. 9: 6-7.

"No: really?" said Brian, "This is the first that I have heard of it."

"Then," said Samuel, "we shall certainly go to the Health Officials the first thing in the morning, and you will be able to walk home."

CHAPTER X.

"Jehovah-Rapha" (The Lord That Healeth Thee.)

Brian was so excited at the prospect of being himself once more that, tired as he was, he could hardly sleep. He awakened long before anyone was stirring in the house, and waited eagerly for his breakfast, which he thought would never arrive.

Finally it did arrive, as did Samuel a few minutes later, to ask if Brian had had a good night. In his impatience, Brian could hardly wait to eat his breakfast, but wished Samuel to start for the Health Office at once.

His cousin ordered the car to be at the door in half an hour, and helped Brian to dress, after which he had the invalid carried down to the car.

The cousins arrived at the Health Office, and Brian was carried into a waiting room, where several other sick or injured persons were awaiting their turn to be healed.

When Brian's turn came, he was carried on a stretcher into the presence of the Health Official, a member of the Administrative Body, where he was set down. The Official asked him how he had been paralysed, and when it had occurred. When Brian told him that he had been in that condition for about a year, the Official looked at him kindly, and said that it was too bad that so much time had been wasted unnecessarily. He then said, "In the Name of the Lord that healeth thee; stand up and walk."

Brian felt a sense of power come over him, and with little effort suddenly stood up and felt himself walking quite easily. He halted, and started to thank the Official, but the latter cut him short, saying, "Give thanks to The Lord that healeth thee;"[1] but Brian was already doing so joyfully in his heart. This caused the Official to smile at him in a very friendly way, and Brian realized that his thoughts were being easily read.

The Health Official then said, "Wait here a minute. I am bringing the Medical Officer who was in charge of your case here for questioning."

---

[1] Exo. 15: 26.

Suddenly the Medical Officer, very dazed and flustered, appeared standing before the Health Official.

Blinking his eyes, the Medical Officer asked, "What has happened? Where am I?"

The Health Official said, "You have been brought here for questioning. Did you treat this man for paralysis?"

The Medical Officer glanced at Brian, and a gleam of recognition came into his eyes.

"Yes," he replied.

"Had you not been advised that The King's orders were that all cases which could not be cured by medical treatment were to be brought for healing to the local Health Office?"

The Medical Officer stammered something about not being able to remember whether he had received this order, but the Health Official gazed at him sternly and said, "Speak the truth;" and Brian realized that the Medical Officer's mind was being read.

The Medical Officer replied, "Yes. I did receive the order, but we were giving him the very best treatment."

"That is not the case," said the Health Official. "When you found that you could not cure him, you preferred to leave this man helpless and paralysed for the remainder of his life rather than to allow The King to have the honour due to Him for healing him. Your heart is not right. Justice must prevail in the Kingdom; therefore this man's paralysis will come upon you and remain with you for a similar period to that in which you allowed him to remain paralysed by your selfishness.[1] At the end of that time you may go to the nearest Health Official for healing, and you will give thanks to 'The Lord that healeth thee' then."

The Medical Officer asked, "How shall I know when the time is up?"

"Calculate from the date when you knew that you could not cure this man until today, when he was healed," said the Health Official. "If you honestly make a mistake in your calculations, no harm will come to you; but if you try to evade part of your

---
[1] I Cor. 6: 2-3.

punishment, it will be doubled. Remember that The King knows all thoughts, as He has always done,[1] so do not try to evade His sentence on you."[2]

As he finished speaking, the Medical Officer crumpled up and fell to the ground, and almost immediately the two attendants who had carried Brian into the office opened the door and came in. They deposited the Medical Officer on the stretcher which had been Brian's, and carried him out of the office. No word had been spoken throughout, and it was apparent that the Health Official and his attendants used some kind of mental telepathy.

Brian walked lightly from the Health Office, and ran down the steps to meet Samuel, who was awaiting him in the car. Samuel greeted him with a happy smile, saying, "Thank The King: I see that you are completely healed. Get in and we shall drive home."

"Not at all," replied Brian. "I shall take your advice of last night, and shall walk."

"Good," said his cousin. "I shall join you," and he dismissed the car.

They started off at a good pace, and Brian said, "But Samuel, surely you should be going to your office."

"Oh, that doesn't matter," Samuel replied. "Everything runs so smoothly now, that my presence is not necessary. If there are any important letters or documents for my signature, they can be sent to the house. There are no business worries nowadays, except that it is very difficult to keep a staff, as everyone wants to move back to the land."

"Now that the money incentive has almost disappeared, nearly everyone having realized that the 'money mania' was due to the propaganda of International Finance, as stated in their protocols; the public now place health, contentment, and happiness, ahead of money-making, and consequently are returning to the land in large numbers."

."The King has stated that the land is His,[3] which everyone admits, and He has divided it amongst the Tribes, so that every

---

[1] Matt. 9: 24; 12: 25; Luke 5: 22, etc. [2] Deut. 1: 17. [3] Lev. 25: 23; II Chron. 7: 20.

individual is now entitled to a small acreage free as a gift from The King."

"With the increased sunlight, and the fact that this increased sunlight reflected from the moon, has made the moonlight as strong as the sunlight was formerly,[1] vegetation now grows very, very rapidly, and hence it takes but a short time to grow a crop. Consequently a man may have his allotment of land free, and due to the speed with which crops grow, he requires to have saved very little money to keep him until his crops come in, when he becomes self-supporting."

"As there are now no weeds or thistles, and as insect pests can no longer eat the crops; also as grain and other crops now command a good and just price as they did before International Finance had obtained control, the farmer's life is a very easy and comfortable one, with the result that I am continually losing members of my staff."

"As you are no doubt aware, the populations of London and other cities are decreasing rapidly owing to the movement back to the land, and I have no doubt that within a comparatively short time large cities will be a thing of the past, with the exception of Jerusalem, of course."

"By the way," Samuel continued, "I have decided to retire. I have far more than my wife and I can ever need, and have no one except yourself to whom to leave it. I have leased a large family holding of land until the next Jubilee, as one can no longer buy land outright,[2] and am going to spend the remainder of my life, I pray, in peace, contentment, and happiness."

"As you are considerably younger than I am, Brian, I considered that you might like to continue my business, as you are at a loose end, in which case I should be only too glad to make it over to you."

"That is really awfully kind of you, Samuel," Brian replied, "and I certainly appreciate your offer. However, I have never appreciated my health and well-being so much as I have today, and have never enjoyed a walk as I am enjoying this one. Really

---

[1] Isa. 30: 26.   [2] Lev. 25: 10.

I do not believe that I could live an office life now, and like yourself and your staff, I want to live in the country."

"I have quite a good pension," he continued, "and could take up my free allotment of land from The King, on which I could live very comfortably, with farming as a sideline. I have a good deal of back pay saved up, as well as over a year's pension, so have plenty to tide me over. I do hope that you will not think that I am ungrateful to you for your generous offer."

"Not at all," his cousin replied smilingly. "In fact I think that you are very wise to put contentment and happiness before material gain. Have you ever thought of marrying, if you don't mind my asking you?"

"Yes," said Brian. "There was a nurse in the hospital of whom I became very fond, but in my paralysed condition I could, of course, say nothing. I shall write her to tell her how I have been healed, and shall see how she takes it. If she seems genuinely pleased, I shall probably return to the Holy Land to see her; that is if she is not being sent back to Britain. I gave your address as the one which would always find me, and she has promised to write me by airmail as soon as she gets her orders for home."

By this time they were turning into Samuel's gate, Brian feeling quite fresh and not the least bit tired after his unaccustomed walk. In fact the health which he had been given made him feel younger than he had felt for years.

On reaching the house, Brian went at once to his room, where he gave hearty and joyful thanks for his restored health and strength.

Soon luncheon was announced, and he joined his cousin in the dining room and enjoyed his meal sitting at a table for the first time in almost a year.

During luncheon, Samuel told his cousin that he had decided to dispose of his business, making over half of the proceeds to Brian and the other half to his staff and requested that Brian accompany him to his office that afternoon to sign the necessary documents. Brian thanked him very deeply, but said that he did not know what he could do with so much money, as his needs were very modest.

After the meal had been concluded, they drove to Samuel's office, where the necessary documents were duly prepared and signed, Samuel stating that he had recently received a good offer for the business, which he had accepted that noon over the telephone.

On their return to Samuel's home, Brian found a cablegram awaiting him, which on opening he found to be from his nurse in the Holy Land, stating that she had been ordered home and to expect her very shortly.

When he communicated this good news to Samuel, the latter said, "She must be fond of you to take the trouble to cable instead of writing. I think that I shall soon be able to congratulate you, so let us have a glass of wine to toast your prospective bride;" and he rang for the butler to bring wine.

The wine warmed their hearts, and Samuel said that one could now understand the meaning of the command, "Go thy way, eat thy bread with joy, and drink thy wine (Yayin) with a merry heart; for Jehovah now accepteth thy works:"[1] as worries were a thing of the past now that The King had set up His Kingdom.

"How very different it all is from what one was taught by the ecclesiastics," said Brian. "What do you think put them so far off in their ideas?"

"Principally Satan's lies," his cousin replied. "Satan's chief work was to keep man from believing and practising Jehovah's Truth. Hence he worked on the minds of the ecclesiastics through the so-called 'scholarship' of his 'synagogue of Satan' to lead them astray from Jehovah's Word, and instead to believe and teach their own ideas of what God's Word SHOULD have said. The result was that man's ideas were taught to the people by the great majority of the ecclesiastics, whilst those ecclesiastics who attempted to remain true to God's Word were outnumbered and outvoted by the infidel majority. The people accepted the

---
[1] Eccles. 9: 7.

teachings of their religious leaders, as they considered that it was their place to know God's Truth, whereas had they themselves studied God's Word, they would have known that He had warned us, 'To the Law and to the Testimony: if they speak NOT according to this Word, it is because there is no Light in them:'[1] whilst Messiah had told us that He is the Word,[2] and also the Light.[3] Hence, by following the teachings of these infidel ecclesiastics, Israel were led astray from the Word and the Light, and instead believed Satan's lies, thus remaining under his system and control."

"Again, the incorrect translation of the Greek word 'Kosmos' as 'world' also put the ecclesiastics off," Samuel continued. "'Kosmos' means 'world-system.' The King's statement to Pilate, 'My Kingdom is not of this world-system;' (Kosmos)[4] had been translated as 'not of this world;' hence the ecclesiastics had stated that it was in Heaven and not on earth. The King had also said, 'I pray NOT for the world-system (Kosmos), but for them which Thou hast given me"[5] whilst He had long before stated, 'The Lord's portion is His People (Israel); Jacob is the lot of His inheritance;"[6] thus stating who had been given Him. Still again, The King had stated, 'They are not of the world-system (Kosmos), even as I AM NOT of the world-system.'[7] In each of these cases, the translators had translated 'Kosmos' as 'world' instead of 'world-system,' thus leading the ecclesiastics astray. The world-system is Satan's system, and entirely contrary to Jehovah's system as given to Israel, which clearly explains the meaning of The King's remarks."

"There are two words translated as 'world' in the Authorized Version of the Bible: 'Kosmos' meaning world-system, and 'Oikoumene' meaning 'inhabited earth,' as used in the judgement of Revelation 12: 9, which states in part, 'And the great dragon was cast out (of Heaven), that old serpent, called the Devil and Satan, *which deceiveth the whole world*'." (Oikoumene, i.e., inhabited earth.)

"Unfortunately the translators showed no discrimination in

---

[1] Isa. 8: 20. [2] John 1: 1, 14. [3] John 8: 12. [4] John 18: *36*. [5] John 17: *9*. [6] Deut. 32: *9*. [7] John 17: 16.

the use of these different words, and the ecclesiastics spiritualized it to mean that the Kingdom was in Heaven, in spite of God's Word to the contrary, and in spite of all the prophecies as to the setting up of the Messianic Kingdom in the Holy Land over the actual Israel Nation of the Twelve Tribes. However, no mistranslations nor false theories of men have the least effect on the carrying out of Jehovah's plans as given in His Word, as we have seen."

"Again, the fact that Satan is a liar and the father of lies,[1] and that he wins all his battles by lies and deceit has not been sufficiently emphasized by modern religious leaders. Probably they were afraid of hurting his feelings. The statement, 'That old serpent, called the Devil, and Satan, which deceiveth the whole world,' had not been considered, nor the people warned of it by modern ecclesiastics."

"We were told that the 'serpent was the most subtle of any living creature,' and probably his most subtle act was to have his 'synagogue of Satan' teach the Modernists through 'scholarship,' that there was no personal Devil or Satan. This teaching they passed on to their congregations, with the result that the latter believed this lie of Satan's, and hence made no attempt to fight against a personality whom they had been taught did not exist. Satan's power and subtility were entirely too much for man, and it required the return of The King to overcome him."

"Still another one of Satan's lies which also led the clergy astray, was one of the ones perpetrated by the Papacy, who stated that God had cancelled His promises to Israel, and had given them to the church, of which they stated that Rome was the true church. After the Reformation, the clergy did not examine this statement nor compare it with God's Word, but instead gladly accepted the statement of the Papacy that the promises to Israel had been transferred to the church, which was, of course, entirely contrary to St. Paul's statement that the Law, given 430 years after the promises to Abraham, could not disannul those promises to Abraham,[2] Isaac, and Jacob, which were given for a faithful act by Abraham."[3]

---

[1] John 8: 44. [2] Gal. 3: 17. [3] Gen. 22: 16.

"Having accepted this false premise, the clergy were forced to think out all kinds of theories to fit the false situation, but they never seem to have realized that Jehovah would keep His promises to the literal Israel, the descendants of Abraham, Isaac, and Jacob, and would set up the Kingdom of God in Israel, as He had promised to do in so many of the prophecies, and particularly as stated by Messiah, who said plainly enough, 'I AM not sent but unto the Lost Sheep of the House of Israel.'"[1]

"It would appear that the ecclesiastics had tried to make a meaning out of the word 'church' which is not in accordance with its true meaning. The Greek word translated as 'church' is the word 'ecclesia,' which simply means a 'called out assembly' or 'called out ones.' The Hebrew word of the same meaning in the Old Testament is translated as 'congregation': further in Acts 7: 38, St. Peter's reference to the Israel 'congregation' is translated as 'church in the wilderness,' (showing that the translators saw that it had the same meaning as 'church'). St. Peter here was referring to Israel, called out of Egypt by Jehovah."

"We can therefore see that Jehovah's promises to Israel had always applied to the literal Israel, which was corroborated by St. Paul when he stated, 'And so all Israel shall be saved.'"[2]

"This was well understood by the Apostles who, after Messiah's Resurrection were taught for forty days of the things pertaining to the Kingdom,[3] and then asked, 'Lord, wilt Thou at this time restore AGAIN the Kingdom to Israel?'[4] As we all know now, the Church, who kept faith in God's Word and in the Name of His Son Jesus as 'God Our Saviour,' are now the King's (Administrative) Body;[5] whilst Israel are His Bride."[6]

"But," said Brian, "I had always thought that on The King's Return, everyone was to be judged."

"Oh: I think that it was quite clear," Samuel replied, "that the judgement on His return was only of the sheep and goat *nations* as such.[7] It was necessary to destroy nationally the 'seed of the serpent' or goat nations in order that they should

---

[1] Matt. 15: 24; 10: 6. [2] Rom. 11: 26. [3] Acts 1: 3. [4] Acts 1: 6. [5] Eph. 1: 23. [6] Hos. 2: 19-20; Rev. 21: 9, 12. [7] Matt. 25: 31-32.

have no national power against the 'seed of the woman' or sheep nations."

"The King is very just and merciful. He knew that Satan was too powerful for man, and that he continually deceived man by his lies. Satan therefore had to be bound and made powerless before man had any chance against him, and this The King Himself did by overcoming death by His Death and Resurrection. As we are told by St. Paul, 'Forasmuch then as the children are partakers of flesh and blood, He also Himself likewise took part of the same : that through death He might destroy him that had the power of death, that is, the Devil.' "[1]

"No : The only ones who have been finally judged to date are the members of His Administrative Body. They had accepted His Blood for their cleansing, and His Righteousness in place of their own self-righteousness, and had carried out His orders on the subject. Hence they were judged as being partakers of His Righteousness, and therefore received spiritual bodies like His, and over them the 'second death' has no power,[2] at the end of the Millenial Kingdom."

"We can see His great mercy in finally judging no other individuals until Satan had been bound, and they could therefore show their own true characters, *not being led astray by Satan's lies.*"

"It is apparently only at the end of the Millenium, after a thousand years of The King's rule during which Satan is bound and powerless, that the judgement of the individual takes place. Hence man, freed from Satan's power and lies, can reach great heights under The King's rule. Everyone now knows that The King is The Lord Our Righteousness, and therefore must accept Him as such, and not depend on their own righteousness. Evidently those who do accept Him as The Lord Our Righteousness have their names written in The Lamb's Book of Life,[3] whilst those who still cling to their own self-righteousness are judged by their own works at the end of the Millenium, and are destroyed, as Satan will again deceive them at the end of the thousand years."[4]

[1] Heb. 2 : 14.   [2] Rev. 20 : 6.   [3] Rev. 20 : 12.   [4] Rev. 20 : 15.

"The King had said to those who rejected His Word, 'The Word that I have spoken, the same shall judge him in the last day.'[1] Hence Gog and the beast system,[2] as well as the false religious systems who placed a church or man in place of The King and His Word as the final authority, and which are referred to in prophecy as 'Babylon,'[3] were, as systems, judged by His Word and automatically destroyed by the 'Brightness of His Coming'[4] when He returned, as His Coming dispelled their darkness."

"There would appear to be some intermediate judgement, as explained in The King's parable of Dives and Lazarus,[5] because we are told that 'There is a great gulf fixed' between the justi-fied and the wicked dead. However, as we are told that The King visited Hades whilst His body was in the tomb,[6] and freed such of the spirits in prison as would accept His Righteousness, this gulf was probably bridged by His Death and Resurrection, as He justified all who believe on Him."[7]

"I think," Samuel continued, "it is made quite clear in the Scriptures that The King wishes everyone to be saved who possibly can be saved. Hence His Mercy in finally judging no ordinary individual until that individual has had every possible chance. It was very different with the teachers of the false systems, which had to be destroyed in order to allow the average individual every possible chance to know the Truth."

"It is also quite clear that at the end of the Millenium, Satan must again be loosed to test the nations.[8] Again, he deceives Gog and Magog, or rather their descendants, into believing that his world-system of war, lies, cruelty, and greed is the correct one, and they again will rebel against The King's rule, and attempt to make war on Jerusalem and Israel. This time, how-ever, Jehovah destroys them completely by fire from Heaven,[9] after which Satan, having been given every possible chance, is cast into the 'Lake of Fire,' and then the judgement of the indi-vidual takes place."

"After this judgement of the individual, in which those who

1 John 12: 48.   2 Dan. 7: 1-28.   3 Rev. 17: 1-18.   4 II Thes. 2: 8.   5 Luke 16: 26.
6 I Peter 3: 19.   7 John 11: 25.   8 Rev. 20: 7.   9 Rev. 20: 9.

are judged by their own works are destroyed,[1] only those
who have accepted the Lord Our Righteousness in place of their
own righteousness having had their names written in The Lamb's
Book of Life, and are therefore, on account of HIS RIGHT-
EOUSNESS, given eternal life."[2]

"All sin having thus been removed from the Kingdom, God
then comes down from Heaven and takes over the Millenial
Kingdom from His Son Jesus, so that 'God may be all in all.'[3]
He then makes the new Heaven and the new earth, which remain
forever."[4]

"But," said Brian, "why should those who have been judged
by their own works be destroyed?"

"On account of 'original sin'," Samuel replied, "ever since
Satan caused the Fall of Eve, and through her, the Fall of Adam,
Satan has in some way had control of man and has been able
to deceive him, and make him feel enmity towards Jehovah, his
Creator. In other words, Satan has caused man to follow his
own example."

"This was first shown by Adam immediately after the Fall,
when he hid himself from Jehovah, saying, 'I was afraid, because
I was naked, and I hid myself.' "[5]

"Prior to the Fall, it would appear that Adam had felt no
fear of Jehovah in that sense, but had rather felt a childlike
love and respect for Him as Father. Since the Fall, Adam was
afraid because he was naked, not only physically, but he had
also lost his robe of Innocency and trust in the Righteousness
of God."

"We can see this attitude of fear even in St. Peter, when he
said, 'Depart from me: for I am a sinful man, O Lord.' "[6]

"Since the Fall, man has been afraid of Jehovah and has tried
to hide himself, or to work out his own righteousness, which will
NOT take the place of the Righteousness of God, as the fear
and enmity are still there in the mind of the worker of self-
righteousness. As St. Paul says, 'Therefore by the deeds of the
Law there shall no flesh be justified *in His Sight.*' "[7]

---

[1] Rev. 20: 15.   [2] Rev. 20: 12, 15; 21: 27.   [3] I Cor. 15: 28; Rev. 21: 3.   [4] Rev. 21: 1.
[5] Gen. 3: 10.   [6] Luke 5: 8.   [7] Rom. 3: 20.

"This fear or dread has caused separation from Jehovah, the source of both spiritual and physical life, so that spiritual and then physical death has resulted. It is the 'enmity against God'[1] which can only be overcome by the Holy (Healthy) Spirit given freely to all those who accept the Righteousness of God in Jesus Christ, Who by His Cross, 'slew the enmity.' "[2]

"The acceptance of the Righteousness of God restores to man the Innocency which Adam had before the Fall, and also slays the 'enmity' or fear, so that the believer again becomes a son of God, as Adam was before the Fall;[3] and therefore once again inherits Eternal Life, as was Jehovah's original plan for Adam."

"On the other hand, the person who trusts in his own works can never overcome 'original sin,' and although he may to outward appearances live a very good life, still he has the 'enmity towards God' in his mind, and is therefore separated from God, which causes death. However, as Satan is now bound for the thousand years of the Millenial Kingdom, and there is no one to deceive man's mind by lies; and as everyone now knows the Lord, it would be only the most pharisaical of men who would still prefer self-righteousness, and who would again be deceived into trusting in works when Satan is again released at the end of the thousand years."

"After the thousand years of peace, health, prosperity, and blessing of The King's Rule, every true Israelite by blood or by faith will prefer that rule, and apparently all of them are true to The King, none of them joining Satan's rebellion, as St. Paul tells us, 'And so all Israel shall be saved.' "[4]

"Yes," Brian replied. "One can see that Israel, having been delivered from Satan's lies, has already realized that her God and King has a second time led her through the 'wilderness' during the 'Times of the Gentiles,'[5] and has brought her into the Promised Land: that His Plan for her had always been one of peace, blessing, and prosperity, but she had instead believed Satan's lies. However, she will never again err in that respect, as the prophecy has been fulfilled which states, 'For they shall

---

1 Rom. 8: 7.   2 Eph. 2: 16.   3 Luke 3: 38.   4 Rom. 11: 26.   5 Luke 21: 24.

all know Me, from the least of them to the greatest of them, saith the Lord, for I will forgive their iniquity, and I will remember their sin no more.'[1] Surely Israel may now say, 'Mercy and Truth are met together: Righteousness and Peace have kissed each other.' "[2]

"Quite so," Samuel said. "The prophecies are all quite clear to us now, and the Anglo-Saxon-Celtic race, having regained their ancient name of Israel, are at last fully aware of its meaning and its blessings. (Israel, i.e., ruling with God.) They also understand the meaning of the prophecy, 'They shall sit every man under His Vine (Israel, Jer. 2: 21: Isa. 5: 7) and under His Fig-tree (Judah, Jer. 8: 13; 24: 1-10) and none shall make them afraid.'[3] It is also quite clear that the prophecy has been fulfilled which states, 'In the place where it was said unto them, Ye are NOT My People; there it shall be said unto them, Ye are the sons of the Living God.' "[4]

"Have you realized," Samuel continued after a pause, "that the nation has been praying 'Thy Kingdom Come' for many centuries, but only very half-heartedly. The ecclesiastical teachings that in the Kingdom the citizens sat on thrones or on clouds, and continually played harps, did not appeal at all to the average person. Actually he did not wish to spend eternity in that manner. In fact, as one prominent man stated a few years ago, 'When we pray, "Thy Kingdom Come," we add a proviso in our minds 'but not just yet, as I prefer my present mode of life better'."

"Had the ecclesiastics searched the Scriptures, and 'Rightly divided the Word of Truth,'[5] they could have visualized what the Kingdom meant from all the prophecies concerning it, and taught accordingly, with the result that the nation would have prayed wholeheartedly, 'Thy Kingdom Come'."

"However, the preaching of the Gospel of the Kingdom was to be one of the signs immediately preceding the Return of The King,[6] so it would appear that only the Gospel of Salvation was to be preached until the 'Times of the Gentiles' was ending."

[1] Jer. 31: 34. [2] Psa. 85: 10. [3] Micah 4: 4. [4] Hos. 1: 10. [5] II Tim. 2: 15. [6] Matt. 24: 14.

"In any case, it took Gog's attack to awaken the nation to the fact that she needed Divine help to save her, and which forced her to make her truly national 'enquiry,' as called for in Ezekiel,[1] with the wonderful results of peace, health, prosperity, and blessing, and above all, that we know The King from the least of us to the greatest of us, which, as the King Himself stated, means, 'And this is Life Eternal, that they might know Thee the only True God, and Jesus Christ, Whom Thou hast sent.' "[2]

"What a wonderful future Israel has before her now! What a difference from the chaos, bewilderment, and sufferings of the years before she made her 'enquiry!' "

"It took a great tribulation to awaken Israel from her self-sufficiency, but Isaiah had long ago prophesied, 'For when Thy Judgements are in the earth, the inhabitants of the world will learn Righteousness.' "[3]

Samuel lapsed into silence, and both sat wrapped in their thoughts, forgetting the worries of the past, and looking up the broadening road into eternity, with the figure of The King in front of them, ever leading them on to higher joys of peace and blessing.

Here let us leave them until Israel makes her national 'enquiry,' when we shall join them in the Kingdom with The King to lead us safely into eternity.

---

[1] Ezek. 36: 37.   [2] John 17: 3.   [3] Isa. 26: 9.

"The Good News of the Kingdom, however, will be proclaimed throughout the whole Empire, as a witness to all Nations: and *then* the end will come." Matt. 24: 14. (Fenton Translation.)